PHANTOMS OF THE SHAH

DANA DUTHIE

Matchstick Literary
1-888-306-8885
orders@matchliterary.com

PREFACE

Although the third book published, "Phantoms" is actually the second of four in the Air Force career of the hero, Brad Mitchell. This series of books, "Phantoms of the Shah," "Tremble," and "Dark Rain," are certainly fiction, but they are based on my 24 year career flying jets in the U.S. Air Force. Many of the characters are based on real folks, folks that I flew and served with. Some of the hijinks described actually happened, and the locations are really there. Chapter Seven describes a lot of the "real life" Air Force, at least as it was in 1978. "Phantoms" is written in the first person for no other reason than to be different.

The situation in Iran today, and our relationship with the Iranian military is certainly different than that described here in the late 70s. Makes one wonder what the world would be like had the Shah stayed in power, or at least the radical Muslim factions not been successful in taking over much of the world of Islam.

"Phantoms of the Shah" is dedicated to the men and women of the 50th Tactical Fighter Wing and the 10th Tactical Fighter Squadron, folks whom I worked and flew with twice in my time in the Air Force. Both units are "retired" now, their heritage and history locked away in a vault somewhere in the bowels of the Air Force Historian facility, or donning the walls of other units formed with the same numerical designation.

PROLOGUE

I am Air Force Captain Brad Mitchell. I am on my third assignment in the Air Force, flying the F-4 Phantom out of Hahn Air Base in Germany. After graduating from flight school at Moody AFB, Georgia in 1969, I took an assignment as a "plowback," an instructor in flight school at Laughlin AFB, Del Rio, Texas. I spent two weeks at Moody after getting my shiny silver wings to get re-qualified in the T-37, the Air Force's primary jet trainer. I had of course flown the aircraft in my own flight training, but had then moved on to the T-38 for my final training of about six months. I had to get re-familiar with the "Tweet," as we not so affectionally called the T-37. Another description of it was the "6000 pound dog whistle," because the engines made an obnoxiously loud shriek, enough to make anyone deaf. What's that you said?

I spent three years at Laughlin and worked my way up to a position as a flight examiner or check pilot, mostly flying with other instructors, giving them check rides. I was also the wing "spin pilot." The Tweet was a rare aircraft in the Air Force fleet that could actually be recovered from a spin. Most other aircraft, once they were in a spin, were almost impossible to recover. It usually meant the pilot had already ham-fisted the plane enough that it was time to jump out of it. The Tweet could easily be put into a spin and the recovery method was a by-the-numbers maneuver that was taught to students. Instructors were required to go through one spin ride per year where they practiced spins and recoveries from several different conditions.

I did well enough at Laughlin that I was able to get a flying assignment next. Because the war in Southeast Asia was winding down, the Air Force found itself with an excess of pilots. Those coming up on assignment were offered the "good deals" of a job at just about any base they wanted, but not in the cockpit. They called it "Rated Supplement," and it consisted of ground pounder jobs in supply, security police, transportation, personnel - all kinds of exciting jobs that I never joined the Air Force to do. I said they would have to take me with my feet dragging. I wasn't going to volunteer. As it turned out, our base got one flying assignment for the whole wing for the year 1973. Our Wing Commander selected me as the recipient and I was very thankful to get a Forward Air Controller (FAC) job in Thailand, flying the OV-10 Bronco into Cambodia to finish up the war.

The FAC mission was important and a lot of good experience. Unfortunately for me, it was short. We shut down the U.S. participation in Cambodia in August, 1973. Although I did manage a few combat sorties and one high intensity mission flying convoy cover over the Mekong River, most of our flying for the rest of my one year tour was training in Thailand. Once again I got very lucky. I had moved up to flight commander and check pilot and was selected with my roommate, Pete Trask, to lead the fleet to Korea, closing down the OV-10 mission in Southeast Asia. It was an interesting four day trip that took two weeks, and when we got back to Nakhon Phanom, Thailand, Pete and I had just four days to go before we left the country. I was destined to fly the huge C-5 cargo monster at Dover AFB, Delaware, and Pete was assigned as a missile control officer at Grand Forks, North Dakota. Luck played a factor again when I was selected to represent our squadron of pilots with what we considered lousy assignments at an interview with the four star general commanding all the U.S. forces in Southeast Asia. I was armed with a list of all of our pilots, what they wanted on their Form 90 "dream sheet," and what they got for assignments. The general was chagrined that the AF personnel system was basically using the FAC force as filler for the assignments nobody else wanted. He was able to change my assignment to an F-4 to Hahn, as well as a few other jobs for the guys. However, he was not able to change Pete's missile hole job - at least not yet. Pete went to Grand Forks and paid his dues, but when he came out of there, his personnel folder had been "red tagged" for a good assignment, and he got an F-15 to Bitburg, Germany. After finding out about my change of assignment I bought the bar for 3 straight days until we left.

I spent a month at Holloman AFB, New Mexico going through fighter lead-in training in the AT-38, and then six months at Homestead, AFB, Florida in F-4 training. I arrived at Hahn in March, 1974. The rest follows.

CHAPTER ONE

NATO LAKE

We were a two ship of F-4Ds, the "hard wing" version of the Phantom that was the mainstay of the U.S. Air Force fighter bomber force during the Vietnam conflict and beyond for many years. The F-4C and D were the predominant Phantoms at first, but they had no internal gun, so the gun was carried in a pod under the belly. That took up space and created drag. Later the "E" model F-4 eventually replaced the "Ds" with a gun in the nose and it was the "soft wing" version. It had slats in the wings that allowed it to turn a much tighter circle, something we found was important in the Southeast Asia conflict up against Mig 21 Fishbeds that could easily out turn the Phantom in a dog fight. The ability to turn inside the opponent's circle meant the Mig could eventually get to the rear and solve a heat seeking missile or gun equation for the kill.

I had my normal weapons systems officer (WSO) in my back seat, Jim "Rhino" Reiner. On our wing was Jay "Bosco" Bostwick, with his GIB (Guy In the Back), John "FUBAR" Cray. Now - if you don't know what "FUBAR" stands for, you might want to

1

read a different book. Oh, alright, it means F%$%#@ed Up Beyond All Recognition. Anyway, we were tasked on a two-ship attack mission against a simulated command post on the north edge of a lake about 100 miles north of our base. Our simulated ordnance was 6 Mark 82 five hundred pound bombs each. We were participating in the 50th Tactical Fighter Wing's North Atlantic Treaty Organization (NATO) Tactical Evaluation (TAC EVAL) in June, 1976, flying out of Hahn Air Base in Germany.

USAF units in Europe went through three major evaluations every couple of years. There was a Management Effectiveness Inspection (MEI) that was mainly a paperwork drill. After all, the motto in the Air Force was "when the paperwork weighs as much as the airplane, you could go fly." Certainly then, the paperwork had to be correct. Inspectors were from the US Air Forces Europe Inspector General team (USAFE IG). It was usually a boring exercise for the aircrews, although we always had to take tests evaluating our knowledge of the mission and our aircraft. The most important aspect evaluated was what was called the Personnel Reliability Program (PRP). Especially in a nuclear tasked unit (which the 50th was), PRP was very important. It meant that training and mission conduct had to be perfect. There were no grey areas in the nuke business. Inspections either yielded an A+ rating or an F.

The USAFE IG also conducted an Operational Readiness Inspection (ORI) of all of its units periodically. This was the mother of all inspections and was usually a wing commander's report card. Pass with flying colors, and the colonel could likely find himself in line for stars. Fail, and he would definitely be in line for the next flight home. The ORI included all aspects of the flying squadrons' tasking from ground attack and air to air, to the nuclear attack mission. It was conducted with the wing in simulated combat gear, including gas masks, and usually concluded with a simulated all out nuclear launch. Aircrews flew bombing missions on the local ranges and simulated missions against targets selected by the IG team.

The final inspection was the one we were flying in today - a NATO TAC EVAL. It was conducted by an inspection team from NATO headquarters in Brussels and the team consisted of augmented aircrews from other wings in the area. NATO did not test the nuke business - most of them were not cleared for it, and NATO knew that USAFE took care of that mission. So the TAC EVAL was just a lot of flying and frankly, a lot of fun.

I had briefed a ten second spaced takeoff because we were simulating carrying a 3000 pound bomb load and the standard takeoff procedures did not warrant a formation takeoff. In today's scenario, a trail departure set us up for our tactical formation to fly anyway. It was a beautiful day - blue sky, not a cloud to be seen. Extremely unusual for Hahn weather. The plan was to stay at low level all the way into the target area, pop up for the simulated attack, and then get back in the weeds for the return to base. After all, we were briefed that there were significant defenses around our target and airborne threats to deal with as well. Little did we know.

After sucking up the landing gear on takeoff I held the nose down a while until about 400 knots, then made a hard right turn of 90 degrees. With Bosco about a mile back, that turn allowed him to slide right into the briefed formation. The Air Force evolved through the ages as threats became more sophisticated when it came to formations to fly. Gone were the days of WWII of keeping the flights in tight formations. The goal now was to be very maneuverable and positioned to be able to watch the six o'clock area for Migs and other "bad guys" trying to sneak up behind you. The standard formation now was about 6000 feet line abreast for a two ship and if it was a four ship, the other element would be about a mile back, forming a box. So Bosco was now about a mile off my right wing just a little bit higher than me. Since we were at low level (around 300 feet), it was prudent for the wingman to be a little higher while he was flying formation, checking six, and watching out for the rocks all at once. The flight lead can check the wingman's six o'clock, watch out for the rocks, and do the navigating.

In that first turn Rhino saw a flash of the sun off another F-4 well above us. It was turning into and diving towards us. As we figured, it was a NATO inspector flying in one of our sister squadron's F-4Es. I initiated another 90 degree turn toward the north and pushed it up. Although the soft wing Phantom could out turn the hard wing D model, it was no contest in a sprint. The slats created drag for him and we quickly ran away from his attack. That was one!

As we came up to the Rhine river my eyes were watered when I looked DOWN upon four West German F-104s below us. Now the low level structure in Germany at the time was pretty loose. East of an imaginary north-south line that split the country you flew in a generally southerly heading. West of the line you flew northerly. The idea was to avoid head on collisions, blasting over

4

populated areas, staying out of restricted and controlled airspace (like airfields), and staying above 300 feet. So here we were at *almost* above 300 feet and I was looking **down** on a four ship of Germans. Well - it's their country, I guess they can fly where they want. It turns out these guys also were NATO tasked to intercept us and other of our squadron mates that morning. They immediately started a turn to try and convert on us. Now the F-4D might not have the turn radius of the Mig 21, or even our own F-4Es, but the kraut in an F-104 is lucky to be able to turn that thing around in the same country. It is basically all engine and very stubby wings that generated little lift in a turn. I had pushed the power up and we were doing about 600 knots. Those guys were toast. That was two!

As we approached our target area, Rhino detected two targets on radar at about our one to two o'clock position a little high, possibly trying to convert on us. I checked the flight 20 degrees into them, making the geometry of a rear conversion that much more difficult and left the power up. We saw them trying to swoop down on us and they were going to be late. It was a pair of West German F-4Fs, the military sales version of the F-4E, so they could turn pretty well, but because they started a little late, they rolled out about 8 miles behind us. That was three!

At ten miles before the target I turned us bout 20 degrees away and pulled the power back some. We had speed parameters on the release of bombs and near the speed of sound was not within them. Five miles out I pulled the nose up into a 30 degree climb and glanced out to see Bosco in perfect position. I let the climb slow us down a bit more and then pushed the power back up to full, I looked down, acquired the target, and as I started to roll in I got a windscreen full of a bright and shiny British Lightning jet. He completely over shot me and obviously did not see my wingman. Bosco got a beautiful high angle gun shot that when we looked at it on his gun camera film later, was the shot even our Top Gun weapons guys dream of. That was four!

Then three came back to play. By checking away and slowing down I had solved the geometry problem for the two German F-4Fs. Rhino saw them first and they were getting in position to saddle up on Bosco before he could release his bombs. I called for a jettison of the bombs and a hard defensive break. Bombs on target are never worth losing a wingman for. The target will be there tomorrow, the wingman might not. As it turned out this time, the Germans didn't see me and one of them crossed right in front of me in our defensive turn. He was trying to get into parameters on Bosco. I selected missiles and heard a nice loud growl on the heat seeker as it acquired the Kraut's tailpipes, and I let it fly (simulated of course). I called out the kill over the radio and we got back down in the weeds and headed for the barn. I called for a fuel check and Bosco was a little below "Bingo," which meant it was time to go home.

Five miles out from Hahn we rolled the power back, climbed to traffic pattern altitude, and roared up for the initial approach still in our tactical spread formation. When we got on the ground I noticed the clock. We had been airborne for a total of 35 minutes. It was probably my shortest mission in the Phantom, but I guarantee it was the most action packed. Although I'd logged a little combat time in Southeast Asia as a Forward Air Controller flying the

OV-10, I had never flown a mission like this one today at NATO Lake. At that time I would bet the four of us were the most combat ready as we could be, and Bosco and I were one fifth of the way to "ACE" status.

CHAPTER TWO

HAHN AIR BASE

The wing passed that TAC EVAL with flying colors. Our squadron, the 10th Tactical Fighter Squadron did extremely well on the bombing ranges and most of the simulated missions like ours to NATO Lake were successful as well. A lot of that was due to the very unusual weather conditions. It was clear and sunny everyday of the inspection, a complete anomaly.

Hahn historically has the worst weather in the world for US Air Force bases. That's saying a lot since the Air Force maintains bases in Greenland, Alaska, Korea, and other "garden spots" with shitty weather. The problem was that Hahn sits on a ridge line in the Hunsruck "Mountains" of West Germany, 600 feet higher than other bases. So when everyone else has a 600 foot ceiling (certainly flyable weather), Hahn is in the soup. That's practically a daily occurrence for weeks and months at a time in the winter, and often even in the summer. It was a common occurrence for the weather forecasters to predict weather at minimums for the most experienced pilots (300' ceiling and 1 mile visibility) at about 1300 hours (1 PM). Invariably we would brief up our missions, start and taxi for a 1300 takeoff and sometimes make it. More likely than not however, the weather had rolled back in for the mission recovery and we would have to divert to one of the nearby lower bases like Spangdahlem, Bitburg or Ramstein. Then we would sit and wait for a Blue Goose (yellow school bus painted Air Force blue) to come and take us home. The next day a fresh new set of aircrews would bus back to fly from the divert base and hopefully recover at home.

The weather is the reason why each winter each squadron deploys to Spain, Italy or Turkey for their training, and even that can be dicey. I remember my first year at Hahn we didn't turn a wheel for almost two months, so in March we were going to deploy the 10th to Zaragoza, Spain for some sunshine and good flying. The problem was the weather wouldn't even raise up to minimums, and even though we could actually take off in next to nothing, we had to be able to come back around and land in case of an emergency right after take off. After two days of taxiing out for a 1300 hour take off, and then weather canceling and taxiing back, someone got the bright idea to call for help. So the next day we taxied the whole squadron at once for a 1300 hour take off. In the meantime, a C-130 loaded with dry ice took off from Rhein Main Air Base near Frankfurt and came in for successive low approaches at Hahn. With ground controlled radar (GCA) help, the big Hercules would fly down as close to the runway as the pilots could stand and the loadmaster would open the rear door and toss dry ice out next to the runway. The dry ice would react with the cloud deck and the ceiling would rise, so that when the F-4 flight lead could see the 4000 foot marker down the runway, he would take off. We'd get 6 or 8 jets off that way and the weather would come back down. Around came the C-130 for the next pass. Eventually we got the whole squadron airborne, and now all we had to worry about was crossing into French airspace.

The French were a bunch of horses' derrières when it came to their airspace. When you wanted to fly across or into France you were given a 15 minute window when you had to appear at their border. As you can imagine, in a scenario like the one described earlier, the timing was blown all to hell. It was not uncommon for flight leads to claim radio failure and press on, though that sometimes brought repercussions down through the hierarchy. After all, the French were supposed to be our allies. Invariably they would also run intercepts on our flights to give their Mirage pilots some training. In fact, if we were flying a French low level for a training mission we always had to announce which low level as we crossed into their airspace. If we had a specific scenario we needed to fly for training, we would often tell them we were flying French Low Level #6, when we actually flew #2. Now, if you wanted some realistic intercept training, you would tell them where you'd really be and keep your head on a swivel for a simulated dog fight with a French Mirage.

I remember one French low level sortie Rhino and I flew that had a little bit of everything in it. The weather was absolutely perfect on a beautiful spring day. We were getting a Pave Spike upgrade ride. Scotty "Beam me up" Perkins was the instructor in the other jet, with "Goose" Geesey in his back seat.

Pave Spike is one of the first and best "smart bomb" system in the Air Force arsenal. At that time, if we were really loaded, it would be with two Mk-84, 2000 pound bombs with a laser tracking device in their noses. The jets also had the Pave Spike pod, a long cigar shaped tube with a TV and laser camera in the nose. The idea was for the pilot to acquire the target by pointing at it, usually in a dive. Then the WSO "designates" the target with the Pave Spike pod, and the weapon is released in reasonably good parameters. The bomb's own tracking device finds the laser beam from the pod and "rides" it into the target. It had what we called "bang bang" tail fins that would slam back and forth at command to keep on the flight path. After release, the pilot can pull out of the dive but must make a moderately gentle left turn while the pod still tracks the target until detonation. As you can imagine, a 2000 pound bomb can make a pretty good mess of any target, and the Pave Spike accuracy was exceptional.

Anyway, Scotty briefed we'd fly a French low level out to the coast and he picked a few bridges and buildings along the way for us to practice on. We told the French we were flying a different low level because we wanted to get in some good training without having to fight off a pesky Mirage jet. As we got closer to the coast however, opportunity popped up for us to "shine" a bit. A couple miles ahead was a farmer on a large combine working his field of wheat. Scotty directed "I've got the left, you got the right" and we went blowing by poor Pierre at about 450 knots right on the deck. Rhino watched when we went by as the farmer bailed out over the side of his tractor. Within minutes, right in front was the "target" of our low level - a lighthouse on the coast. Again with Scotty on the left, and us on the right we went screaming by the lighthouse **looking up** at it. Fun!

We spent the next twenty minutes or so out over the English Channel designating and practicing drops on ships. Finally Scotty remembered to check on our fuel. We had all been having so much fun that we let flight management lapse. I was significantly below "Bingo" fuel, a level that left just enough to get back to base and save some for Mom and Apple Pie. Scotty was also very low on gas so he immediately led us into a zoom climb to over 40,000 feet and got a clearance direct to Hahn. Usually we didn't fly that high, but because we were up in "the nose bleed section" of airspace, there was no other traffic and the controller granted the direct heading request. At about 40 miles out from base we rolled the power back to idle and settled right down on initial approach with what was indicated as the same amount of gas as when we started the climb. Rhino and I were impressed. The jet almost "makes gas" when you're up so high.

Hahn had two squadrons of F-4s in the mid 70s, the 10th TFS flying hard wing F-4Ds and the 496th flying the soft wing F-4Es. The 10th transitioned to F-4Es in late 1977 and a third squadron was also formed - the 313th TFS. The 10th and 313th had a primary mission of nuclear attack, with back up tasking of conventional attack and a little air defense. The 496th had a primary role of air defense, with a back up of conventional air to ground attack. There were four aircraft loaded with the B-61 nuclear bomb on alert at all times. Tenth and eventually 313th aircrews would rotate through 3 or 4 day tours on 15 minute alert. There was an alert facility with 10 bedrooms, a common shower room, a dining hall and a recreation room with TV and a pool table. Crews could actually be mobile on the base with a truck and a radio, as long as they could respond and be in the jets with engines cranked and ready to taxi in about 10 minutes (to be airborne in 15). It was not uncommon to be in the base theatre with your family watching a movie when the horn would go off. Folks on base got used to the trucks flying down the roads and taxiways, but the aircrews never got too comfortable with the whole thing. You always wondered, *is this the real thing?* Once the engines were up and running the pilot would check in with the command post. The alert had originated at USAFE headquarters at Ramstein Air Base, so the command post staff were being exercised as well. They would read out a long "message," letters and numbers that would correspond to an exercise message each crew had. If it had been a real launch message the pilot would authenticate it with a "cookie" (code translator), and then all hell was about to break loose. After the exercise message was received, the crews would shut down, re-cock the jet for the next time, and sometimes stand by while it was refueled.

Squadron life at Hahn was as good as you made it. Some folks never got used to the weather. Some wives and families never got used to the numerous Temporary Duty (TDY) assignments to Zaragoza, Aviano, Incirlik, etc., not to mention the days of their men sitting alert and not able to come home. Most folks though made the best of it. Most of the line aircrews lived off base on the German economy. The landlords of the surrounding area knew they had a steady source of income and there were some nice places to rent up to 30 minutes from the base.

We worked hard, but we partied hard too. The Hunsruck sitting astride the Mosel River meant wine country. There were weinfests all the time in the quaint towns along the river. The 10th "married up" with one of the local wineries and we bottled our own brand of Mosel wine. Herr Schmidt would let us know when it was time to pick the grapes in the fall, and we'd invade the hillside with families of pickers. Some would even prance around in the big vats barefooted, crushing the grapes. Then we would help him bottle it and put on our custom wine labels. Of course these sessions also meant a lot of wine drinking as well. It's a good thing white wine doesn't need to age very long … if any. When I left Hahn in 1979, we had just bottled a fresh batch, and even having several parties, I couldn't get rid of it all. So, I wrapped a case of wine in linens and laundry that was packed in my household goods. Then I put 10 bottles in a carry on bag and dragged it aboard with me when I flew into Dulles Airport outside Washington. It was close to midnight when we got in and I saddled up to the customs agent, a rather rotund African American lady, and plopped my bag of wine in front of her, fully expecting to pay the rather steep customs charge for bringing it into the country. She eyed me and said "What chyall got in there honey?" I told her it was ten bottles of German wine. She looked at me and said, "You shittin' me?" Then she looked around to see who was watching and said "Get on outta here." I left a happy man. Trouble was that the case of bottles hidden in my household goods popped its corks during the trip to the states, and I had a rather lush smelling bunch of boxes to unpack.

One basically made the assignment to Hahn a lot of fun and hard work, or a real drag. The latter was often the case for the married guys. Their wives tired early of the lousy weather and the fact that we were out in the boonies, a long way from the land of the "Big BX." That was military speak for a shopping mall. The base had a base exchange (BX) and a commissary, but pickin's were slim. Once in a while there were trips to Ramstein and Kaiserslautern, larger bases to the south with larger stores and more opportunity to spend money. But most folks coped, and in fact the wives often got together and went to the big German cities and stores. There were Christmas bazaars in Heidelberg and elsewhere, and life on the economy wasn't all that bad. It was also common for a few of the more daring wives to get together, rent a truck, and drive to Brugge, Belgium to fill up with antiques. The guys often brought home the specialty items of the area from their TDYs too. Lladro ceramic statues were big in Spain, rugs and brass in Turkey, and butcher blocks in Italy. So, the bottom line was we enjoyed our time at Hahn by working at it.

I remember one party. Actually I don't remember much of it. Can't even tell you who's house we were in. But I remember driving home 30 minutes in dense fog. One of the guys offered to go with me since I was several sheets to the wind. We were in my little red Fiat Spyder convertible. It was cold, sleeting, and the fog was so dense I couldn't even see the road in front of me. My co-pilot, and I'm ashamed to say I don't even remember who it was, hung out the passenger door, looking down, relaying what he saw ….. "pavement, pavement, gravel, gravel, ditch, pavement." That was how we got to my house - me driving at about 30 mph and he hanging out the side letting me know how to correct back to straight.

The little weinfests in each town along the Mosel River were always a lot of fun. A lot of wine too. Invariably they would have a small carnival co-located with the wine booths and brat stands. The carnivals always had bumper cars, and give the fighter pilots and gators a bumper car operation and look out! Usually the German folks were smart enough to stand by and watch when we took the wheels of the bumper cars. There was no mercy given to the nearest "enemy" car.

One of the squadron pilots and his wife had quite an adventure one night during and after a weinfest. She was 9 months pregnant and not a very tall girl. The parking lot for the fest was across the highway from the actual event. It was a four lane highway with a rock wall divider down the middle, about 40" tall. You had to cross the road and climb over the wall to get to the fun. This young mom to be (I won't divulge her name to keep from embarrassing her too much) kinda got stuck straddling the wall. Basically both feet were off the ground. It couldn't have been comfortable in her condition - probably wasn't too much fun for the baby either. Anyway, hubby helped her over and they went about enjoying what was to be their last night of childless fun. He drank a lot of wine while she stuck to Sprite and lemonade. Later that night she jabbed him in the side in bed and announced "It's time to go." He jumped up in a tizzy and ran around in a stupor for a few minutes until she calmed him down. "You call in to the hospital and tell them we're coming. I'm going to take a quick shower. I'm in a sweat."

Our intrepid father to be made the call, got their "go bag" in the car and the car warming up, then went into check on his wife.

There she was, lying in the bottom of the shower curled up in a ball, about to have a baby. Yikes! He was able to get her bundled up in the car and off they went for the normally 30 minute (tonight 20) drive to the base. The nurses met them at the car, put her on a gurney, and almost made it to the delivery room, when the little fighter pilot made a noisy entrance to the world. All was well and we all enjoyed cigars at the bar the next night.

There are as many stories as there are alumni of Hahn Air Base and the 50th Tactical Fighter Wing. We've got time for one more. This time yours truly was the "hero." Hmmmm, maybe "villain" is a better term. Anyway, I was on Victor Alert one day as the Alert Force Commander. We had a new Base Commander on post - a female colonel. Back in the 70s there weren't that many women colonels in the Air Force and those that there were really had their stuff together so they rightfully commanded a lot of respect. Anyway, the colonel wanted to meet a representative (preferably the leaders) of every unit on base in her conference room at headquarters. By way of explanation, fighter wings back then (and now) had a full colonel Wing Commander who was the HMFWIC of the wing. Almost always he was a pilot and he had a Vice Commander (No.2) who was also a colonel and flier. Then there was the Deputy for Operations, a colonel who oversaw all the flying operations, a Deputy for Maintenance who was a colonel in charge of ... you guessed it - maintenance of the aircraft. Everyone else on base, with a few satellite exceptions, came under the auspices of the Base Commander. That included the cops, supply, personnel, logistics, recreation, food services, a hodgepodge of whatever was left to run the base.

Anyway, the lady colonel held a meeting and since I was basically sitting around on alert waiting for the balloon to go up (hopefully not), and since the Squadron Commander wasn't really interested in going to this meeting, I was selected to go to represent the 10th TFS. I took one of the other alert pilots and our back seaters with me and we parked our truck in a fast getaway position in front of headquarters. Never one to be late to a meeting, I got us there early and we filed to the back of the room and took chairs against the wall, leaving the chairs at the table to the bigger muckety mucks. Us fighter crews always tried to keep our backs to the wall - never could tell who might be trying to sneak up on you. The meeting got going and we had just finished introducing ourselves when the horn went off. "Klaxon, Klaxon, Klaxon" loud and clear over my handheld radio. That meant the alert force had been scrambled and we had 15 minutes to get to our jets, crank up and be at the end of the runway, ready for take off.

"Shit!" I said, and because we were basically blocked in the room by about 50 bodies, I led our force up onto the conference table and down to the other end (where the colonel was sitting), off the table, and out the door, our combat boots clomping on notepads, coffee mugs, and a nice centerpiece of flowers. Obviously I didn't get to see how the colonel reacted, but later witnesses told me she was in shock for a minute or two. It turns out she hadn't been briefed by anyone yet as to what happens when that klaxon goes off, and the fact that nothing else on the base matters but what we were in the process of doing. Obviously it was a practice alert and we didn't fly, and I had the "pleasure" of showing the good colonel around the alert facility the next day.

CHAPTER THREE

TDY

When the boys went TDY (Temporary Duty) to Zaragoza they really unwound. The wing at Zaragoza had no aircraft of their own assigned. They had a dozen or so qualified pilots and instructors who manned their weapons office and later came up with an instructor school that all the USAFE units participated in. But the host pilots were dependent on the TDY units to bring in the jets. Most of the time there would be just one squadron on the ramp at once, although often there would be a couple weeks overlap of two squadrons. The flying was mainly based around the Bardenas Bombing Range, although there was also a small island - just a big rock really, where once in a while we could go drop real bombs. The "bombs" we dropped on practice ranges were 25 pound BDU-33s, small, but aerodynamically similar to a 500 pound bomb. We also would carry the MK-106, which was a small bomb that simulated the high drag vertical fall of a nuke under a parachute. We exercised the guns on strafing runs with training rounds - definitely deadly, but not high explosive.

After the day's flying was done, everyone "retired" to the officers club for a round (or six?) and some good fun. We sang every dirty fighter pilot song there was, and even made up some of our own. There was usually a crud match going on at the pool table, maybe a dart tournament, and a lot of "Deceased Insects." The deal there was that if anyone in the bar yells or even says in passing the words "dead bug," everyone hits the deck. The last one down buys the next round. There were other games played for drinks as well, and if you weren't careful, you could blow through your TDY money in a heartbeat.

Crud is a game played with two pool balls - the cue ball as the "shooter," and one other as the target. Teams are formed and the members follow each other, alternating sides in rapid succession taking the cue ball and slinging it against the target ball before it stops rolling, trying to get it in a pocket. Teams alternate shots, so if I shot and the target went in the pocket, the guy on the other team who shot before me loses "a life." The number of lives each player gets is determined by the judge and usually depends on how many are on a team. The judge is usually a senior ranking officer positioned at the middle of the table on one side. The shooter must shoot from the ends of the table, and if he violates that rule and his "valuables" are beyond the end of the table, the judge will call "balls" and that's a life. Of course, if he is a she, then a different term is used. If a player touches the judge in any way, that's a life and he also owes the judge a drink. If the target ball stops rolling before the cue ball hits it, that's a life on the next shooter. It is supposed to be a non-contact sport, but with all the running around to retrieve the cue ball and get back to the end of the table to shoot before the target ball stops rolling, it often gets brutal. At the end, the last man standing is the winner and the other team owes the winners a round.

A typical Friday night for the 10th TFS at the Zaragoza bar goes like this. There's a warm up period where everyone has a drink or three. Then there's "Late Night with Saber One." The squadron commander brings out the bent saber. It's just what it sounds like - a saber from a military school, with the blade bent at a 30 degree angle half way up. The commander awards the saber to one of the guys (or gals) who had highlighted himself/herself rather negatively the most during the week. The recipient must keep the saber in safe hiding all week until next Friday. Relentlessly the LPA (Lieutenants Protective Association) will hunt for the saber all week. If they find it and produce it at the bar during the week, the guardian for that week has to buy all the the lieutenants a round. How demeaning! A typical faux pas that would earn one the Bent Saber might be for a flight lead to not pay attention and not know there was a runway change while he was flying, then bringing his flight up the wrong way to land. Another might be not noticing the wing colonel just walked in while you're standing at the ready room counter stating how you are going to "take him to the cleaners" on the golf course.

After the Saber has been presented and the recipient has bought a round, then it might be time for singing. There are some good and almost clean fighter pilot songs from the Vietnam era, and a lot of raunchy ones as well. This is usually when the Wing Commander's wife or some of the other ladies of the base permanent party get disgusted and leave. All that does of course is raise the volume level, or maybe even launch a round of carrier landings. Tables are pushed together to form a "carrier" with a deck of 15' long or so. Someone finds a hose - hopefully like a fire hose, but even a garden hose will work. The "deck" gets slathered down with beer and a little soap, and the LSO (Landing Supervising Officer), manned with ping pong paddles, declares the carrier open. Usually a couple flight commanders man the hose (the Navy calls it the cable), and the landing "jet" hits the deck belly first and feet up as fast as he can. The LSO commands the "catch." If he waves the pilot off, the cable doesn't catch and the body goes off the the end of the carrier, sometimes into a tub of ice. If the LSO likes the approach, he commands the catch and the "cable" (hose) comes down hard on the back of the jet's legs to be caught by his raised "hook." This usually results in several welts on the back of legs, a split chin or two by hitting the deck too hard, even worse if the Saber is so inebriated he can't catch himself as he rolls off the end.

At least once this activity resulted in a few broken tables and a whole tray full of broken glasses, and the Wing Commander's wife went home and bent her husband's ear something fierce. Soon the squadron was kicked out of the club and the Squadron Commander was summoned to visit the wing king the next morning. Not to be put to bed dry though, the Sabers resulted to hall bowling at their billeting quarters. Someone found a bowling ball left by the last squadron in one of the closets and a ten-pin game was soon set up using San Miguel beer bottles (empty of course - NEVER waste good beer) as the pins in the hall of the quarters. Meanwhile the LPA decided to invert the whole crew quarters. The Lieutenants Protective Association is an informal organization of all the lieutenants in the squadron who believe there's safety in numbers. When they were tired of being the "goats" in the squadron they tried (usually in vain) to fight back. Tonight they pulled an "inversion" by going through every room, turning everything upside down - the bed, the desk, the chairs, the refrigerator (even everything IN the refrigerator). If someone had retired early to bed, unlucky! They usually found themselves up against a wall with their bed on top of them.

So where is all the "adult leadership" you might ask? Obviously if the Hahn colonels are deployed with the squadron, things are tempered a bit. The host unit senior staff pretty much knew when it was time to leave the club. They kind of work under the three monkeys rule. You know - "Hear no evil, see no evil, speak no evil." Or "What I don't know can't hurt me." There have certainly been some squadron commanders or operations officers lose their jobs over some of these hijinks, but for the most part, responsible parties step in just in time and minimize at least the damage.

TDYs to Aviano Air Base, Italy or Incirlik in Turkey are usually not that wild. There are more permanent party folks there and the TDY units have to act more like "guests." Especially in Aviano, and also in Zaragoza there are some great restaurants off base. If Fridays are the rowdy nights at the bar, Saturdays are usually nights on the town. The Sabers had their favorite spots and they curbed their rowdiness as well so as not come off too much as the "ugly Americans." At Zaragoza one of the favorite eating establishments was La Fraguas, a very informal place - didn't even have a sign…. just an old Vespa motor scooter leaning against the wall next to the door. Inside were wooden floors, a long wooden bar and big wooden tables. In the middle of each table was a keg of red wine - Tinto. There were glasses and chalk. Every time you filled up, you marked off on the keg with chalk. The standard fare was "choppers," thin grilled lamb chops swimming in garlic - maybe cabrito, a loaf or two of French bread and a big green salad to share. At the end of the night the waiter added up your choppers and your wine count, and you all threw enough money on the table plus some. In Aviano it was Orsini's, a restaurant out of town on a ridge road. Senor Orsini would seat us all at a big table and take our orders by memory. We could have 20 guys at the table and he'd remember what everyone wanted. He also paired every course (usually five of them) with a different wine. We were well lubricated when we got back to base.

TDYs were a lot of fun and good flying, but most of us were ready to go home, even to the lousy weather when it was over, if for no other reason than to dry out. My last TDY before I left Hahn was as the USAFE liaison for a squadron deployment from the states to one of the German bases. During the spring especially, NATO would hold huge exercises which involved stateside squadrons deploying to what would be their home should the balloon ever really go up and there was a conventional war. On this particular occasion, an F-4 unit from Moody AFB, Georgia (Moody had transitioned out of the pilot training business) flew into to Jever Air Base in northern Germany. I first went stateside to Moody to brief them on the airspace and rules of flying in Germany. Then I was at Jever in the control tower when they came in for their month long deployment. At this time Jever was a German F-104 training base. It's Wing Commander was an old colonel who had been an Ace for the Luftwaffe flying Messerschmitt ME-109s in WWII (Hitler's premier fighter). He took great pride in boasting about how many Americans he'd shot down. It was all in jest and in fact, he was a great host.

Colonel Schmidt led about twelve F-104s out to the end of the runway when I was in the tower waiting for the Moody guys to come in. I had no idea what his plan was, but it became obvious when he was talking to the folks in the tower and they cleared him for takeoff when the F-4s had just crossed into German airspace. The Zippers, as the 104 was affectionately called, roared off, joined up on their colonel's wing, and ran a massive intercept on the incoming flight of 24 F-4s. The American contingent was led by a new Brigadier General Jack I. Daniels, kind of a prude. Anyway, as the Germans completed the intercept and were converging on the General's lead formation, Colonel Schmidt came up on the radio, "American F-4s from Moody AFB welcome to Germany, request permission to come aboard? I'd like to lead you to my base."

There was a long pause and then General Daniels said "Negative" and left it at that.

Colonel Schmidt was flabbergasted, and he tried again. Bottom line - Daniels refused to let the F-104 inter-mingle with his F-4s and they came on in and landed alone .... as did the Zippers.

That night at the German Officer's Club was supposed to be a rousing welcoming party, and for the most part it was. General Daniels and Colonel Schmidt were on speaking terms but that's about it, and Daniels was beat. They had spent close to 8 hours in rubber anti-exposure suits flying on a non-stop flight with multiple refuelings. He retired early to bed. Some of his aircrews should have done the same, but they stayed up trying to out-drink the Luftwaffe in beer and schnapps. Big mistake. The krauts had a tradition of serving what's known as an "Afterburner," - a shot of clear schnapps or Jaegermeister lit on fire. The idea is to down it real fast so as to deny the fire oxygen and the fire goes out. The German pilots were demonstrating very successfully and a few of the yanks did well too. However, several of the Moody guys missed their mouths completely when they tossed the drink down and badly burned their faces. As a result, I got to fly quite a bit in Moody jets around Jever while they had a few crew members on medical Duty Not Involving Flying (DNIF).

We went on several smaller TDYs as well, usually two or four ship formations on cross countries or squadron exchanges. We had an eight aircraft visit with a squadron of French Mirages to Lyon, France one day. We launched off and met them in the middle, rat raced around in a huge simulated dogfight, affectionally called a "furball," and then recovered at Lyon for lunch. The French pilots could never understand how Americans would refuse to drink wine with their gourmet lunch. For them wine was like water and it is the customary "go with" for every meal. But the good old USA hierarchy frowns upon us drinking within 12 hours of flying.

Another time we had a ten jet exchange with a British F-4 unit out of Leuchars, Scotland. We sent ten jets to their base and they sent ten to Hahn. We then spent a couple days flying together, sharing tactics and hijinks. I'll always remember, we took with us a load of Mosel wine in our C-130 support aircraft, and they sent a pallet of single malt scotch whiskey in their bird. We definitely got the better deal on that trip. I mean, Mosel wine is good, but single malt scotch? Hmmm, hmmm. All of us got at least one mission out of Leuchars on a low level over Loch Ness. We made lots of noise and parted the waves, but try as we might, we couldn't raise the monster off the bottom of the lake. I think whoever had seen Ol' Nessy in the past had been partaking in the single malt too much.

The USAF spent lots of money and effort flying and training with our NATO allies. We sent formations to Norway, Denmark, France, Britain, Italy, Turkey …. anywhere we could to become familiar with their forces, tactics and environment. It was good fun, sometimes hard work, and always worthwhile. I'm not sure if that can be said about our trip to Iran in 1978.

CHAPTER FOUR

THE SHAH'S AIR FORCE

Back in the 1970s when Shah Mohammad Reza Pahlavi was in power in Iran, the U.S. and Iran were "friends." Although he had been in charge ever since the middle of WWII and his record of human rights and democracy was less than desired, back then the U.S. wasn't quite as interested in those things. Iran had oil, we needed oil. Iran also was in a conflict with Iraq, a country with a leader we surely wanted to go away. So we outfitted the Iranian military with top of the line equipment - in some cases better than our own Air Force flew. They got brand new F-4Es with the best avionics, F-14 Tomcats equipped with Phoenix missiles, loads of the best munitions in the U.S. arsenal, and a state of the art electronic training range. Those were just the aviation goodies. They scored state of the art tanks and artillery as well.

The U.S. also trained Iranian pilots in the States, both in primary flight school and in follow on training in F-14s. Although some of them did well in their training, many did not. They were first sent through english language school and then straight to pilot training. I flew with a couple of them at Laughlin when I was an instructor there. I also witnessed a few of them do some really stupid things. We always had the opinion that because Iran also had a small pilot training operation of their own in country, they put their best candidates through in house and sent the idiots to the U.S. The policy was we could not wash them out of training, we simply washed them back to the next class. I had one "classmate" in my training at Moody who had been there, stuck in the T-37 because he couldn't land the jet for two years. Later, when I was back there after my own graduation getting pilot qualified in the Tweet, the same student had finally caught on enough that his instructor let him go up solo.

At pilot training bases the Air Force controlled the takeoffs and landings from what we called the Runway Supervisory Unit (RSU), a small glassed in enclosure positioned near the approach end of each runway. It was manned by an instructor pilot and an enlisted recorder. They had radios and controlled the traffic and kept tabs on the day's flying. The actual control tower was manned as well by the normal contingent of air traffic controllers, but about all they did was direct incoming and outgoing aircraft not associated with the training operation.

Solo pilots had last priority when it came to the traffic pattern. Until he was ready to make a full stop landing, a solo student would be lucky to be able to complete a pattern to a practice approach. The RSU controller would use the opportunity to launch those waiting in line to take off by simply sending the solo pilot around for another try. When sent around, the procedure was to stop your descent, level off, add power, raise the landing gear, and parallel the runway to the departure end, and then go around and try again.

This particular Iranian had been sent around three times, twice because his pattern was terrible, approaching dangerous, and once because of traffic. He finally decided he'd had enough and called for a full stop landing to finish his sortie. Once again however, he botched the approach and overshot his final turn and was told to go around on the radio. He kept coming. The controller again told him to go around and cleared two aircraft onto the runway for takeoff. The student kept coming. The controller saw that he was about to cause a catastrophic event, and fired flares above the runway which was always the signal to abandon an approach. This time it worked. The Iranian went around, leveled off at 500 feet, raised the landing gear, and continued north out of the base's airspace. The wing issued a communications search for him, as well as a search through the Atlanta based air traffic control system. About an hour later a phone call came into the base operator from a farmer about 100 miles north of Moody. It seems our intrepid student had remained at 500 feet and continued north on runway heading until he ran out of gas and pranged into the farmer's field, killing himself. Interviews with some of his Iranian classmates indicated he just figured that because the RSU controller kept sending him around, Allah had decided it was not his day to land.

My roommate and I in pilot training had an interesting experience with a couple of Iranian students one evening. We lived in old WWII barracks that weren't half bad - two small bedrooms, a bathroom, a sitting room, and a small kitchen. Trouble was, the buildings were wooden and if there ever was a fire, they would go up in flames pretty quickly. We were studying in our place one night when we smelled something burning, coming from the Iranians' room next-door. We went and banged on their door and when they opened it we saw they had built a fire in the middle of their sitting room floor and were roasting a goat for the two Valdosta State University girls they had brought home. Fortunately they succumbed to pressure and we were able to put the fire out. The girls took that hint to hit the road and the two Iranians were sorely disappointed.

My strangest encounter with an Iranian student was when I was in my last year as an instructor at Laughlin. There was one student who had been washed back a couple of times because he simply would not go through the by-the-numbers steps to recover from a spin. The IPs would have to wrestle the controls from him to recover before they hit the desert floor. Since I was the designated wing "spin pilot," the colonels decided to have me fly with the guy. He was big for an Iranian - not real tall, but muscular, and I was glad the T-37 has a side by side cockpit so the instructor could reach the student if necessary. Off we went, up to about 15,000 feet and I talked him into putting the jet into a spin. As with any other airplane, for it to spin you basically had to run it out of airspeed with a high angle of attack. We pulled it up to about a 30 degree climb, pulled the throttles back to idle, and when the airspeed reached stall parameters, simply stepped on one rudder pedal and it would fall off into a spin. We usually let it rotate a couple of times to experience the aspects of a spin, and then we recovered. I called for the recovery and he just sat there, staring ahead. I took command of the aircraft and recovered with plenty of altitude to spare, then we climbed back up and I would discuss the process again, and again. Granted, my "discussions" became a little more heated the last time, but he never really reacted much. So, we tried it one more time. Nose up into a climb, power back, rudder in at stall speed, and away we went. After two rotations I called for the recovery. Nothing. We had lots of altitude, so I ordered him to recover again. Nothing. This time I yelled at him - "Recover! Stick full aft, Rudder and ailerons neutral, power idle, determine direction of spin, rudder full opposite direction, stick full forward and hold." He got that far this time and we were hanging in the seat belt straps under negative G. The jet would normally stop rotating at that point and transition into a dive from which you pulled out and the recovery was complete. Bozo here though wouldn't pull the stick back to pull out of the dive and we were going straight down, maybe even a little inverted in a negative G dive. I finally took the controls and tried to initiate the recovery. He wouldn't let go, even with my screaming at him. His right arm was locked stiff holding the stick forward. I reached over and whacked his arm, trying to break it loose. Nothing. Finally I reached over and squeezed his oxygen hose so that he got no air. That was enough to weaken his grip and I was able to pull us out of the dive at about 3000 feet. Our minimums for practicing spins were 10,000 feet. Whew! As we flew back to base I asked him what was the story. His answer? "Let the will of Allah be." In other words I guess, if Allah wanted us to recover that day, Allah would have made it happen.

Needless to say, that student didn't make it, although he was still there going through T-37 training when I left for my next assignment several months later. Rumor had it that the reason the diplomats and Pentagon hierarchy refused to allow us to wash an Iranian out of pilot training was that if they went home without their wings and with their tail between their legs, the Shah would have them beheaded for bringing shame to their country. I tried to find out if that was true - a little later here in this story.

CHAPTER FIVE

EXERCISE CENTO ONE

In the fall of 1978 the U.S. administration decided that to shore up our relationship with the Iranian Air Force we would deploy a squadron to Shiraz, Iran to train and fly with their guys in most aspects of our mission - everything but the nuclear mission. Even back then we definitely did not want Iran to have nukes. The exercise was dubbed "Cento I," and the 10th TFS was designated to deploy. We sent the whole squadron of aircrews along with 24 of our F-4E Phantoms. We launched on a questionable but flyable day on the first of November, planning on returning before Christmas. I had just moved to the wing standardization and evaluation office as a check pilot, but because my replacement as flight commander, a new major, was not yet checked out as a flight lead, I lead the second of four six-ship formations. Our squadron commander, Lt. Colonel Mike Watson led the first flight and the whole deployment. He had the wing vice commander (Full Colonel George Harwood) as his number three man. I had basically my old flight in my formation. Rhino was in my back seat. Bosco and Fubar were my number two. Larry "Clit" Katorian was my number three and deputy flight lead. He had Ron "Toad" Heyman in his back seat and on his wing was one our new but very sharp lieutenants, Bob "Boomer" Huston. The other two jets were manned by some of the Fightin' Tenth's best. The final two formations of six were led by the Operations Officer Lt. Colonel Ken "Smooth" Fracelli and Major Tony Gilford, the Assistant Ops Officer.

Our launch went fairly smoothly. We launched the six-ships in 15 minute trail with separate flight plans, but our plan was to form up just north of Shiraz and arrive over the base with a gorilla of 24 jets. We taxied out a spare with the first and third flights and had to sub one of them into Fracelli's flight for a wingman who had a flight control problem prior to take off. We were heavy - three external tanks of gas, weapons ejector racks on the empty pylons, with two baggage pods hanging there. The baggage pod was simply an old napalm bomb body - empty of course - that had a door on the side. We could stow luggage, aircraft chocks, parts, even cases of beer or wine in them (single malt scotch too). Fortunately the pilot could not release them - they were hard wired on. We certainly wouldn't want our underwear and squadron wine spread all over the country side with an inadvertent delivery. And DEFINITELY not that good whiskey.

Because we were heavyweight and the weather was a bit "iffy," I briefed a 30 second radar trail departure for each jet. With a six jet formation that meant my flight was strung out for almost ten miles in the climb out. Once leveled off, I powered back and let the flight join to a loose "V" formation with me in front and Bosco in basically a "fighting wing" formation, back between 10

35

and 30 degrees off one wing and about 1000-1500 feet out. From there he basically had a cone around me within those parameters that he could maneuver in. Because we were on a controlled flight plan with an assigned altitude though, the wingmen basically needed to stay at approximately the same altitude as their leaders. The other two flights of two were spread out between 30 and 45 degrees off my wings in the same formation about 4000 feet out. That way, we were all in sight of each other and I could maneuver as necessary without having to worry about them needing to fly a tight formation. If we came up on any weather or reduced visibility, I would rock numbers two, three and four into a wingtip formation on me and number 5 and 6 would join up tight and fly in one mile radar assisted trail behind me.

The French were fairly amenable today, mainly because we all made our designated 15 minute windows to cross into their airspace. They were a little chagrined when our last six ship wasn't completely aboard - still catching their leader when he entered French airspace. But Tony Gilford had been around a while and he knew that all the Frogs could really do was croak. He pressed on and his flight joined when they were good and ready. The French did manage to scramble a couple of their Mirages to run an intercept on us. Rhino and I watched as a two ship of F-1 Mirages botched an end run on our flight and rolled out 7-9 miles back. I was saving gas, so I only pushed it up a little bit to make it more difficult, and eventually they came within about 500 feet of my lieutenant wingman. The Frog flight leader then came up on the radio with a typical French attitude and accent, "Aah American F-4 flying over Lyon, thees is Mirage F-1 Dubois Flight, request

36

permission to join." Since he was already within our space, I simply acknowledged by saying, "Be my guest Monsieur, but be careful of the flight of two now closing on your left wing." They obviously had not even seen our outboard flight on the left wing and had managed to sandwich themselves. Too bad our missiles weren't hot. Frenchy obviously immediately looked left, pulled his power back, and they disappeared down and behind us.

We air refueled twice off of American tankers. The first was a flight of two KC-135s flying out of Zaragoza Spain. The second was two KC-10s that had launched out of Aviano Air Base, Italy. The first refueling track was just after we broke the coast of France over the Mediterranean. The second was just before we entered Turkish airspace. Air refueling a larger than normal formation is not a problem as long as one of the chicks is not significantly lower on gas than the rest. If that's the case, the flight lead puts him on the boom first. Today, we had plenty of gas if we missed refueling, to divert to Zaragoza for the first rendezvous, and Incirlik, Turkey for the second. I simply rocked the flight to close in to a loose route formation on me with numbers two, three and four off my right wing, and numbers five and six off the left. After I took my gas I slid to the left outboard of number six while number two took the boom. He took his gas and slid under to the left and onto my left wing, and so on. It is all done with minimum radio chatter, leaving that to the boom operator to give corrections as each jet maneuvered to position. The tankers have what are called director lights under their bellies to aid the pilot to maneuver to the correct position forward and back and side to side. We had a round of drinks on a bet to see who could get on, take fuel and get off with the least chatter from the boomer. Ideally you would hear "cleared to contact number one," "contact" once the boom is in the slot, and "disconnect" once you've filled her up. A lot of that depends on how chatty the boomer is. We'd all had had a hook up or two in the last month, one of the many squares we had to fill every six month cycle. Unfortunately though, we were not always lucky enough to have the modern tankers to hook up with over Germany. Often Air National Guard units would deploy to Europe from various stateside units with old KC-97, four engine propeller driven tankers for their training as well as ours. That was always a challenge. The KC-97 would have to be flying as fast as it could while we were practically at stall speed in the F-4 to hook up. Sometimes, if we were sporting three external tanks and our refueling time was right after takeoff, we'd be so heavyweight we would have to lower the flaps to keep the angle of attack within reason, and even pull one engine back while shoving the other into minimum afterburner, fanning the speed brakes to match the tanker's airspeed. That took a lot of rudder finesse as well. So by the time we got on the boom on this deployment it was a piece of cake. We thought!

CHAPTER SIX

WELCOME TO IRAN

We had one more air refueling session when we crossed into Iranian airspace. We'd been briefed that they had their own tankers that they had retrofitted from airliners. The U.S. did not want to sell Iran the ability to spread their power too far, so we did not sell them any KC-135s or KC-10s. As we crossed Turkish airspace we started to close up the spacing amongst our flights of six. We wanted to be able to join up with Colonel Watson's flight and all appear over Shiraz on his wing. I had closed to within eight miles of his flight when he joined up with the Iranian tanker. It was a KC-747, a huge jumbo jet rigged with a boom and a basket off the wings. The Navy and the Iranian F-14s used the basket to refuel. The Air Force uses the boom.

We were briefed that the director lights under the tanker's belly were different and in fact might not work at all. That obviously was a problem. The other surprise was that the boomer was a "boomette" - a woman. Now we had refueled with female boomers in our Air Force and they were generally very good. This one was very good too, just not what we expected from this Muslim country. Anyway, Colonel Watson had minimum issues getting his gas, as did most of his wingmen. However, his number three was the Vice Wing Commander and I guess he'd had trouble refueling off the American tankers as well. It turned out he had only refueled once in the F-4 and that was two years ago. Fortunately he had an instructor pilot in his back seat on this mission, so that made him legal, and the IP was able to talk him through the first two hookups. This time however, the immense size of the tanker and the lack of any guide lights gave them fits. The boomer was very gracious. She kept calling off directions, "forward 20, down three, etc." but neither the colonel nor his IP could make contact. I had joined the fray by then, sitting a mile back with my six ship. After a few more vain attempts, Colonel Watson, always one to throw the BS flag, called off the flagellation going on under the boom. He sent Colonel Harwood and another wingman to Tehran to land, gas up, and join the squadron later.

Now it was my turn. I slid up under the belly of the beast and was overwhelmed. It seemed like I had an entire windscreen full of aluminum. When I got to where I thought was the right position I called, "One's ready." The boomette said with almost a chuckle, "No number One, move forward 20 feet." then it was "Now, move up four feet." This went on for a little while and when I was really uncomfortable underneath and what I assumed was way to close, she said "Stabilize.....contact," and we got our gas. Fortunately I didn't lose too much face because everyone in the flight had the same issues. In fact, by the time the tanker had finished refueling the whole squadron (minus the two in Tehran), we were only about a hundred miles from Shiraz.

We managed to join up the gorilla and soon we had company. A four ship of Iranian F-4s ran an intercept on us and Colonel Watson gave them the lead to take us on in. We all joined on the boss' wing in fingertip with eleven on one wing and ten on the other. We flew over the base that way while the Iranians pitchout and landed ahead of us. Then Colonel Watson started an easy turn back to parallel the runway and we fell back into four ships with about two miles spacing behind him. He brought us back up initial in an echelon formation each and one by one we pitched out and landed behind the boss with about 5000 foot spacing. Each of us hustled down the runway to make room for those behind and since it was a 13,000 foot runway, it was not a problem. We turned off at the end, stuck our tail feathers away from the taxiway and jettisoned our drag chutes. Our maintenance folks were already there, having deployed in a C-141 stratolifter that morning. We all shut down together and expected a welcoming committee with at least a beer. Not to be. Although Iran was not the serious Muslim country they became later, they still had prohibition in force.

As it turned out though, there was a nice reception for us at their officers club later with delicious food and even a few libations to go around. Very few of their squadron aircrews were there however - just a few of their ranking officers. As we were to soon find out, the rank and file aircrews in the Iranian Air Force maintain a very rigid demeanor. They work hard, but unlike the Sabers, they didn't hardly play at all.

CHAPTER SEVEN

SOME EXPLANATIONS

As I review what I've written so far, I realize I owe you, the reader, a few explanations and descriptions of Air Force terminology. All this vernacular is natural to me, and to probably most of the readers, but I'm sure it might be a bit complex for a few. So, let me try to explain.

First you'll notice I use the term "knots" or nautical miles per hour instead of our standard miles per hour. That is standard aviation terminology, though I'm not sure why. It is a naval term from way back. Suffice it to say that one knot = 1.16 mph. So, if we say the wind is blowing at 30 knots, it is howling at about 34 mph. When we fly our traffic pattern at 300 knots, we're doing 345 mph, and when I say I've pushed it up to 500 knots to get away from a bad guy, I'm doing about 575 mph (approaching the speed of sound). By the way, the speed of sound, often referred to as "the mach" or "Mach One" varies based on altitude, temperature, and atmospheric pressure. At ground level it is somewhere near 600 knots.

When I referred to slats on the F-4E, I meant the sections of the leading edge of the wing that extend and lower to create more camber over the wing and thus more lift. You have seen slats when you sit in the window seat of an airliner over the wing.

The standard Air Force traffic pattern for fighter aircraft or formation coming in to land is either a straight in approach, (often flown as an instrument approach and sometimes under radar control) or it is an "overhead pattern." Overheads consist of an inside and an outside downwind leg of what is essentially a rectangular box pattern. Normal procedures are to enter the pattern at the prescribed altitude and airspeed onto the outside downwind, flying the opposite direction of the operational runway heading. The jet or flight will turn a base leg ninety degrees to the runway heading, and then onto the "initial" approach. Initial is flown over the runway at pattern altitude (say 1500 feet) on runway heading. If in a formation, the leader will put the wingmen on his wing opposite the turns to be made in the pattern. At a specific point about halfway down the runway, the pilot or leader "pitches out" banking into a 45 to 60 degree turn of 180 degrees, slowing down, and rolling out on "inside downwind" going the opposite way. Wingmen will take 3 - 5 second spacing on the pitch out, rolling out in trail of their leader. On inside downwind the speed is reduced and the landing gear and flaps are lowered and checked for down and locked indications. Depending on how tight a pattern the pilot wants to fly, and sometimes depending on other traffic, the pilot rolls off "the perch" onto a descending "base" turn. Most fighter pilots like a nice tight turn, so they'll roll out on final approach about 300 feet in altitude and 1/2 mile out, aiming to touch down in the first 1000 feet of the runway. In the F-4 we had a drag chute to deploy after landing to help slow down, and it would be jettisoned in a designated area after clearing the runway.

I talked about weather minimums for a landing. Minimums depend on the weather, the pilot's experience, the equipment on the aircraft, and usually the guidance of the higher ups. Normal weather minimums for an experienced pilot in an aircraft that is not flying a "coupled approach" are no lower than 300 foot ceiling and one mile of visibility. A coupled approach is one where the aircraft basically flies its own approach "coupled" to the equipment on the airfield and can sometimes be flown down to a much lower altitude with the pilot simply monitoring the controls to take over if necessary. The Navy flies a modification of a coupled approach when they make their carrier landings. Airliners and big transports often make coupled approaches. Regardless of how the minimums are determined, when the altitude (300 ft?) is reached, the pilot must be able to see the runway enough to make a safe landing. Otherwise he is required to make a "missed approach" and go around to try again or divert to an alternate base.

The formations we flew to Shiraz were described. Basically there are four different formations we flew in the Air Force. "Fingertip" formation is the one you see the most as aircraft fly overhead. It is depicted by the fingers on your hand (minus the thumb). Notice the middle finger is the one up front. That's the leader. Number two in the formation is the pointer finger. Numbers three and four are the ring finger and pinky. In a close in fingertip formation the wingmen fly with about a 3' wingtip clearance. It is a maneuverable formation but the leader needs to be smooth as he rolls in and out of turns. If you've seen the Thunderbirds or the Blue Angels fly you were witnessing fingertip formation at its finest.

"Route" formation is fingertip but with more spacing - usually a wingspan or more. It is more comfortable and thus more maneuverable, but still not very tactically efficient. The wingmen are spending almost all of their time flying formation and very little time looking at their instruments, radar, or outside for the bad guys.

"Fighting wing" is a formation like I described for my number two man on the way to Iran. The wingman is back in about to 30-60 degree cone around the leader about 1500 feet out. It is a very maneuverable formation and the wingman can slide to the inside, outside, wherever he needs to as the leader turns, climbs and dives. It still does not provide for much defensive coverage to the rear and for that reason, it's usually used as an offensive formation.

Finally there is a "tactical" formation. Tactical is a catchall phrase for just about any formation the leader wants to fly in a tactical scenario, be it ground attack, air defense or other activity. I briefed a "line abreast," about 6000' out for our NATO Lake mission. If it's a four ship, the "Box" formation is simply two line abreast elements with a mile or so spacing. That is a good formation for ground attack missions and affords optimum coverage of the 6 o'clock. Air to air or air defense flight leaders might brief a version of the box with the wingmen (#2 & 4) in more of a fighting wing position. Suffice it to say that a tactical formation is whatever the flight lead briefs.

Most of the time we wanted to make as few radio calls as possible. Directing formations to specific positions could be called over the radio ("Two, go to route," or "Flight go tactical"), but the comm out method is used extensively. To call a formation into fingertip the leader simply rocks his wings gently. To move them out to route formations he flutters the rudder pedals, fishtailing the jet. To send them to tactical he simply porpoises the jet. To cross the flight to the other wing the leader dips his wing in that direction. So for example, if a flight enters the traffic pattern as a four ship, the leader will normally have them in fingertip or route formation at that time. As he rolls out on initial, to set up for the pitch out, the leader will dip his wing to the side opposite the upcoming pitch or turn. The wingmen slide down, back, under, up, and forward to the "echelon" formation - with all the wingmen on one side.

A little about refueling. I described the director lights on our tankers. They are pretty straight forward. In essence, inflight refueling is simply flying formation. The boom is just what it sounds like - a boom about 20-40 feet long and 8-10 inches in diameter. On the end toward the customer there are "wings" that the boom operator uses to maneuver the boom a little bit, and a nozzle at the end. In the F-4 and most Air Force fighters there is a door, usually behind the cockpit that covers a receptacle about 4-5 times the size of the gas tank receptacle on your car. The pilot opens the door, flies the jet to a position beneath the boom, and the operator plugs the hole with the boom. "Contact." You're taking gas. The pilot, the boomer, and the elements can disconnect it when refueling is complete or if the parameters of the boom and jet are exceeded (rough weather, ham fists, etc.).

You might be wondering about the abundance of nicknames we seemed to have for each other. There's, Bosco, Fubar, Smooth, etc., so far in this story The use of nicknames or "tactical call signs" is a time honored tradition in the Air Force - the whole military world for that matter. Who knows when and how it started, but I recall the Red Baron was the nickname of Baron Von Ricktoffen, the famous German Ace from World War One. Another name in the history of the Air Force probably best describes how a call sign may have come about. General Carl Spaatz was the first Chief of Staff of the U.S. Air Force. His nickname was "Tooey." Get it? "Ptooey" Spaatz. There was probably a spittoon around somewhere.

Tactical call signs were used extensively in the Air Force, Navy and Marine aviation. The Army helicopter folks used them as well, especially during the latter parts of WWII, Korea and early in the Vietnam War. An example would be that "Buick Flight," a call sign assigned for a specific mission of the day, would be made up of a four-ship of fighters. The leader might be named "Lobo," since his last name was Wolfe. Number Two might be "Lucky" because he was from Las Vegas. Three might be "Hoss" because he was a big guy from Montana, and Number Four might be "Pig Pen," because he was kinda sloppy looking. So, there you have it - Lobo, Lucky, Hoss and Pig Pen flying today as Buick Flight. When they talked to each other on the radio in the early Vietnam days they would use the individual nicknames. That tradition ended a little bit later when a wingman forgot his flight lead's name in the heat of an air battle when calling for a defensive maneuver. The leader was shot down by an encroaching Mig and he spent the rest of the war as a guest in the Hanoi Hilton. Call signs were verboten from then on and individual pilots were simply "One'" or ("Lead"), "Two," "Three," and "Four."

Nicknames made it back in the vernacular later, especially at overseas bases, but they are not used to identify individuals of a formation. The flight leader might sometimes use his nickname as the call sign for the flight as filed in a flight plan, but he would still be "One" or "Lead" to his wingmen. For example, I gained my "tactical call sign" or nickname well after my tour at Hahn and trip to Iran when, I was the squadron commender of the 80th Tac Fighter Squadron in Kunsan, Korea. I was dubbed "Conan," because the Conan the Barbarian movies were popular then, and the squadron decided to nickname their leader after the star of the show. The fact that I'm 6'4" and weighed about 225 might have had something to do with it too. Anyway, I might lead a four-ship as Conan flight, but I would still be "One" or "Lead" to the wingies.

In Korea these days, the process of assigning nicknames and "tactical callsigns" is a standard ritual soon after the flier arrives on base. Once there were a few "nameless" newbies on the base, it would be decided that it was time for a "Sweep," or mass invasion of a few of the bars in the shanty town invariably located outside the front gate. The whole squadron would make the rounds of a few favorite bars, and at one of them the "Old Heads," or experienced members soon to rotate back to the States, would go through the process of assigning nicknames to the new folks.

Sometimes it took a real stretch of imagination to figure out how the name was derived, but in most cases that nickname would stick with the pilot or weapons systems officer for the rest of their career and beyond. A good example is Bob "Boomer" Huston. He got the name "Boomer" one night at Hahn during a squadron basketball game against another unit. Bob came down with an offensive rebound, and at 6'4" went right back up and two-hand slam dunked the ball. "Boom!" yelled the bench, and from then on he was Boomer. That stuck throughout his long Air Force career, through his second career working for a defense contractor, and until this day. He is and will always be "Boomer" to those who know him best. There are lots of other call sign stories - at least one for every monicker, but I can tell I'm starting to lose you now.

Ok. Enough ground school. You are ready to step to the jet to fly. There will be a test later. Suit up and I'll meet you in Iran.

CHAPTER EIGHT

SHIRAZ, IRAN

One interesting note to start. Did you know that Shiraz wine actually was discovered in and around Shiraz, Iran? The Australians probably produce the most of it today, but the original grapes were found on the hills around Shiraz. Funny though, we weren't served any.

The time in Shiraz was interesting in many ways. We got a lot out of the flying, mainly because we got to drop live bombs and shoot live missiles that we hardly ever got to do in Germany, or anywhere in the USAF for that matter. The U.S. gave so many munitions to the Iranian Air Force (IAF) that they had huge stockpiles - more than they ever would use in their conflict with Iraq. As a consequence, on almost all of our missions to their bombing ranges we used live munitions.

But the flying was frustrating too, especially at first. The IAF had very strict and regimented rules and policies they followed. Virtually everything from the formations to fly to the radio calls to make was dictated from above. The squadrons, and especially the individual flight leads, did not have the luxury to vary from some very stringent tactics and regulations. That became very obvious to us on our first sorties with them. We always flew in four ship formations - two IAF F-4s and two USAF F-4s.

On my first sortie I flew as number three in the four ship with Rhino in my back seat and Boomer Huston and his weapons systems officer, J.J. Romanski on our wing. The Iranians were in the lead and number two aircraft. That was a good idea we thought, so that they could show us around and get us accustomed to the local airspace and environment. For the next mission we switched roles with the same personnel. I led and the IAF crews were numbers three and four. In both missions the scenario was the same. We had dropped the centerline fuel tank and baggage pods on our jets and just had the two wing tanks and weapons ejector racks. So we loaded up 6 live Mark-82 500 pound bombs each.

The IAF flight lead was a major in their squadron and a flight commander. He had 6 full aircrews in his flight, much like we do in our squadrons. For this mission he had a very experienced WSO in his pit (backseat) and an experienced captain and WSO in the number two jet. His briefing was long - almost two hours. I thought part of that was simply because he wanted to explain everything to these American crews to be sure there were no questions and deviations to the policies. For the first mission we didn't mind too much, though we sure could have used a coffee break after an hour or so. What we found out though was that every mission the IAF pilots led, the briefings were the same - very detailed and regimented. It became obvious that the wingmen in their air force weren't supposed to have minds of their own, but were expected to fly pretty much by the numbers.

Major Hassan briefed fingertip formation all the way to and from the gunnery range. The range was 250 miles north, about 100 miles southwest of Tehran. We had the pleasure of meeting our favorite boom operator in their KC-747 tanker on the way home to Shiraz, soon after departing the range. As it turned out, we refueled off that huge tanker several times during our six weeks. We almost got used to it completely dominating the wind screen, and were able to speed up the process after one or two refuelings. I didn't think too much about the formation we were to fly before we stepped to the jets. I guess I thought he would loosen it up to at least a route or maybe a fighting wing once we were airborne. I didn't expect the Iranians to fly the same tactical formations we did, but I planned on briefing and deploying it when I led.

We took off in ten second trail and in full afterburner which was appropriate since we were carrying live munitions and fairly heavyweight. Rather than have us join up straight ahead or at least on the climb out en route, Hassan used the join up technique that is taught in pilot training. The leader starts a turn after accelerating to climb out airspeed and the wingmen use the cutoff to join in the turn. It is appropriate at altitude after maneuvers and to get the flight together before descending to land. But the turning rejoin basically means the leader will do a full 360 degree turn before heading out on his mission, and if there is a cloud deck to stay below, he will end up blowing right through traffic pattern of the airfield. Anyway, we joined up and were in tight fingertip formation all the way to altitude and all the way to the range - some 250 miles. We descended to the range and he led us up the bombing approach heading in fingertip and echelon formation and pitched out for our individual attack patterns. That was the first time we could relax, just in time to concentrate on our bombing.

Their bombing range was amazing. More targets with concentric circles and more tactical targets (tanks, trucks, bunkers, etc.) than we had ever seen on any one range before. Even the great bombing ranges around Nellis AFB in Nevada weren't equipped like this one was. We were briefed and flew a box pattern and dropped one bomb at a time, three from a 30 degree dive using the pilot's manual sight, and three from a 20 degree approach using "dive toss," a radar assisted delivery that the WSO does from the rear cockpit. The pilot actually "pickles" the bomb and starts an easy recovery, and the bomb releases when the jet reaches the parameters the radar commands. Then we dropped down and strafed with the gun from a box pattern and a 10 degree dive. When we were done, the leader went into his climbing turn and we were directed to rejoin to fingertip again. Upon rejoin, each wingman took a look at the jet ahead of him to be sure there was nothing hanging there (like an ornery bomb) that wasn't supposed to be. After number four was aboard, number three dropped down to check him over. That is standard procedure for the USAF as well.

Fingertip all the way to the tanker. Fortunately Hassan moved us out to route (by radio call) when he was about to saddle up for fuel. But just as soon as we were all gassed up, it was back to fingertip all the way back until on initial at Shiraz. I was exhausted. Concentrating on tight formation positioning is tiring. I actually moved out to a route position once and kicked Boomer out as well, but as soon as Major Hassan saw that he commanded us to tighten it up over the radio. He didn't say anything about it in the mission debriefing. In fact, he didn't say much of anything in the debriefing. It was very short. We never even reviewed our gun camera film or discussed the bombing scores. I held my tongue (not a usual thing for me), deciding that we were going to do things differently when I led.

That was the next day - same aircrews, same scenario. I planned on a briefing to start an hour fifteen before takeoff, and we went about our mission preparation after arriving at the squadron building about 30 minutes before that. As soon as I walked in I noticed Major Hassan and his crew sitting in the briefing room, obviously waiting to start the briefing. I made them wait. I briefed a straight ahead rejoin after takeoff, and I had to repeat that when the number four man asked if we would turn first. I briefed that Boomer would join on me, that Hassan would close to a one mile trail and number four would join on him. Then I briefed we would go to tactical formation comm out. I would porpoise my jet and Boomer would break out to the side to about 6000 feet line abreast. When Hassan saw that he was to signal his wingman to do the same and we would fly a box formation to and from the range and the tanker. After our rejoin, Rhino noticed that although Boomer was in perfect position, Hassan and his wingman were a mile back but in fingertip. I gave him a little while to be sure he had seen Boomer's break, and then I called "Three and Four, go tactical." The response I got was "Three," but no movement. I tried again - same response. I tried one more time after we left the tanker - same thing. As we neared the base for our recovery I decided to just leave him back there and rocked Boomer aboard before the pitch out. Hassan decided as we got close that he should bring his element up and join on his own. I let him do it without saying anything, deciding it would be an interesting debriefing. I was pissed though. You NEVER joined on another aircraft without permission. Sort of like boarding a boat without the captain's permission. It just isn't done.

We got back in the squadron building and I sat everyone down with a TV and our gun camera films - I thought. Turns out neither Hassan nor his wingman turned their cameras on, even though I had briefed to do so upon pitching out on the range. So we reviewed my film and Boomer's, analyzing the different actual parameters and results. Rhino spent a good bit of time on the dive toss analysis. Since we didn't have film to work with for the IAF guys, we simply guessed at what might have been an error resulting in a miss. Number four's scores in particular were not so good. However, I couldn't tell if he understood or even cared why. He just sat there and never said a word. When I'd ask him a question, he would simply say "Yes sir."

So I critiqued the formation, re-briefing what I had wanted, thinking maybe Hassan simply didn't understand. I asked him if he had and he said "Yes." So I asked why he didn't fly the briefed tactical positioning. He responded that it wasn't an authorized formation for them to fly. I decided to let the higher ups deal with that, but I did suggest to Hassan that the tactical formation allows for good visual lookout, and that they might want that in their conflict with Iraq. I suggested that an Iraqi plot could easily sneak up behind them while they flew their fingertip formation. His response? "They wouldn't dare." Hmmm.

Colonel Watson did have several conversations with his counterpart squadron commander (also named Hassan) about tactical formations, and finally after about four weeks, we got them to loosen up and fly what we briefed. We also worked on some tactical range work, flying a low level pattern and popping up to deliver our ordnance. That too took a little persuasion. I got the feeling they were not comfortable flying at low level. At first they played the same game if we briefed a low level mission. I might brief a box formation on the low level, and we'd look back to see them up about a thousand feet and in fingertip. We certainly didn't want to force them down in the weeds if they weren't comfortable. After all, in our own training of new guys, we utilized a "step down" approach to low levels and higher minimums for inexperienced plots. These guys all had over 1000 hours in the F-4, but I would characterize them as "inexperienced." Again, as we got toward the end of the deployment, the IAF aircrews loosened up their regimen and their bombing scores even improved.

Along with bombing missions to their main range we also got to fly with and fire the Maverick missile, a munition we had just received at Hahn, and only a few of us were checked out in it. The Maverick is a "tank killer" and we actually got to fire two of them apiece at tanks and trucks on one of their other ranges. The missile basically has a TV camera in it. The pilot rolls out aiming with the bomb sight at the target. The Maverick is slewed to the sight at that point. Uncage it and the camera is locked on to the target, and unless something goes wrong, it blows the target's shit away. That's the definition of a "smart bomb," or in this case, "smart missile." The IAF also had a fantastic electronics countermeasure range. It was equipped with all the latest Soviet weapons radars. As we flew through it, our radar warning receivers would light up and chirp specific sounds. It was great training to be able to identify when we are being "painted" by an enemy weapon. If we had an electronic countermeasures pod, it would activate to try and break the lock of the targeting radar. To be sure, our squadron aircrews benefitted greatly from this deployment. We just thought it was a shame that we had to go and use some other country's equipment to practice with our own U.S. munitions.

CHAPTER NINE

DOWNTOWN

Although our maintenance folks and enlisted airmen in the squadron were all billeted on base at Shiraz, the aircrews were put up downtown in what they described as a "luxury" hotel. Enlisted folks in the IAF are considered peons and treated like dirt. Fortunately we knew that before deploying down there so we brought several large tents to erect in a field close to the aircraft. So our maintenance and other enlisted folks had individual cubicles with nice cots, a large dining hall and recreation set up. They even had a saloon tent with a bar and pool tables. We didn't bring the pool tables, so I'm not sure where the guys "procured" them. In fact, I don't think anyone even asked.

The Shiraz Bandas Hotel was close to the center of the city. There was adequate public transportation (busses and taxis) to get around town, but not to get there from the base. We basically chartered a bus to make four round trips a day so that we could get to the base in time to brief for the morning mission or stay in and make the afternoon go. The last bus out to the hotel left at 7 PM. The hotel had a passable dining room that tried to serve "American fare." They served a decent breakfast of eggs, breads, and fruits. Lunch and dinner meals consisted of lamb burgers, naan or pita breads, pizza with lamb or goat, and some ethnic Persian cuisine. There were also a few restaurants within walking distance of the hotel. There was a good Indian grill and a couple of Chinese places. We were not restricted in our movements downtown, but we soon saw that our presence was not appreciated by everyone. Our military hosts were friendly enough, but for the most part they didn't socialize - at least not with the Americans. Younger males on the streets were the most daunting, especially when they traveled in groups. Iran was going through turbulent times and the radical Muslim factor was decidedly anti-American.

The IAF had a gym on base with a basketball court, so we tried to get up a game or two with our hosts. For the most part they weren't interested, so we created an informal league made up of aircrews and our own maintenance folks. We had four teams and played a round robin tourney twice a week. We also had brought with us some baseball equipment (bats and balls) and we "borrowed" the use of their cricket field. Persia was never part of the British empire, but the British did own the oil back in the early 1900s, and the spread of cricket as a national sport that was prevalent in neighboring India and Pakistan, spilled over into Persia as well. We figured we could teach them baseball (softball) and they could teach us cricket. That didn't go over too well, and neither did our trying the American version of football. We quit trying to convert our hosts to our sports and just satisfied them by trying to come up with a soccer team that could give them a good match.

The Shah was not in country at the time. He had been diagnosed with Leukemia and was abroad in France for treatment and relaxing in one of his many homes around the world. For most of the time we were in country he was in his mansion in Monte Carlo. He had been in power for almost 37 years, and for most of that time he had ruled with a powerful, yet relatively humane hand. Women were not shunned and were allowed to wear western clothing. They didn't drive yet, but they were educated, and in fact almost 70% of the Iranian populace had at least a high school education.

Although the Shah was a Muslim, he was not a fanatic about it, and that pissed off many the Ayatollahs and Mullahs in the country, especially in and around Tehran. They had been successful over the past couple of years creating turmoil, especially in the young male population. University students were staging sit outs and demonstrations, women were harassed, and foreigners, especially Americans, were confronted by groups and mobs. There had been no violence yet, but many of the pundits thought it was just a matter of time.

In Shiraz things were much calmer. Although there was a large university and the students often expressed their feelings in demonstrations, the military had a strong hold on the community. Along with the air base, which was huge, there was an army base and there was a "national guard" which had originally started as the Shah's version of our Secret Service. The Shah had a palace in Shiraz as well as three others in the country. Because of the turmoil in Tehran, he usually stayed in Shiraz when he was in country. He also had been a pilot and kept his own fleet of aircraft on the base. The base commander was a two star general in the Air Force, Rajid Ranjahni. His son was a senior captain in the squadron we flew with. He was Janil Ranjahni and he had been one of my students when I was an instructor at Laughlin AFB in Del Rio. "Jani" as we called him, was one of the good sticks. He probably would have received his pilot training in country except for the fact that at that time his dad was the colonel in charge of their training operation, and he wanted his son to get the best training available.

As I said, Jani was a good student and in fact we hit it off very well at Laughlin. It was obvious he was different than the rest of his Iranian classmates. His social status was that of a VIP and most of his other countrymen stayed away from him. I noted that he had a temper as well, and witnessed him severely flog one of his classmates one day near the Laughlin Officers Club. Evidently the kid had failed a check ride that day and Jani was not happy that he was bringing shame upon his country. Jani loved to fish and I had bought a 16 ft bass boat that I used a lot on Lake Amistad, on the Rio Grande River. I took him out a lot and it was great! He always bought the beer. When I saw Jani in Shiraz we continued our friendly relationship. He had married and had a couple kids, and he had me over to their house several times for dinner and of all things — cocktails? It seemed that Jani and his father had acquired quite a taste for single malt scotch and I was never one to turn down a wee dram now and then. It was during one of these nights out that I questioned Jani about the fate of Iranian students who washed out of our pilot training and were sent home. He wouldn't give me a straight answer and when I just came out and asked if they were beheaded he changed the subject. I took that for a "Yes!"

I met Jani's father too. In fact I flew with him. He was qualified in the F-4 and evidently flew once a week or so. When we got involved with trying to teach his pilots tactical formation, it was obvious the authorization for them to break tradition had to come from the top. At least on Shiraz AB, that was Major General Ranjahni. He decided he wanted to try it first and to the chagrin of their squadron commander, the general wanted to fly with me. His son evidently had told him I was his favorite instructor at Laughlin and that my bomb scores on the range were better than any of theirs. So, since I was an instructor pilot, I flew in the general's back seat on a four ship low level range mission to one of the closer in ranges. We were #2 on Lt. Colonel Watson's wing and numbers three and four were Jani and my old friend Major Hassan. Hassan had his normal GIB in his pit, but Jani wanted to fly with Rhino. I had told Jani about how good a WSO Rhino was and he wanted to see for himself.

The mission went well. Colonel Watson briefed the comm out signal of porpoising his jet to send us to tactical formation and then pushed his nose over to dive down to low level (500 feet). General Ranjahni made a gentle turn away and rolled back even about 1500 feet out. The boss had briefed 6000 feet. I asked the general if I could take control and he said yes. I rapidly cranked the jet to 60 degrees of bank, cobbed the power up, and then, when we approached a mile out, jerked it back to parallel the leader. He didn't say anything but flew a descent formation, even at low level. Turns out he was better down there than most of his

IAF pilots. Rhino said the same thing about Jani. In fact, he said he had to comment a couple times that they were "getting a bit low." On the range the general was very good. Colonel Watson had briefed a low level to pop up deliveries, three using manual (iron sight), and three with dive toss, followed by two strafe passes. Now I flew in the pit quite often as an IP, but I was lousy at dive toss on the radar, so I very diplomatically suggested the general use manual bombing for all six bombs. He ended up with 4 of 6 "shacks" (bullseyes) and 53 hits on the strafe rag. The only one in the flight any better was his son, Jani. He was 6 for 6 on target with his bombs and had 64 strafe hits. Of course, Rhino helped a bit there - he used dive toss on the last three bombs.

When we rejoined after the range work and checked each other over, the boss called for tactical formation again. This time the general racked us to about 80 degrees of bank, yanking 4 G's and rolled us out perfectly line abreast about a mile off the leader's wing. I recovered from having my helmet smashed against the side of the cockpit and cheered "all RIGHT sir!" When we came back to land, General Ranjahni asked me if I wanted to make a back seat landing. Since I was actually almost out of backseat currency I said yes and we asked Colonel Watson if we could make a touch and go before our full stop landing. He agreed and in fact the whole flight did one touch and go. My pattern was ok. I had to step on the rudder a bit to get us lined up on the runway and I basically made a Navy "take that runway!" touchdown before taking off again. The general took the jet then and made the smoothest landing I had ever experience in the F-4. In fact, I used the old saying "are we down yet?" as we rolled out to the end of the runway. He was that smooth.

That night General Ranjahni invited Colonel Watson and I over to his beautiful house for drinks and dinner. It was a bit awkward, because he did not invite Colonel Harwood, our Vice Commander. In fact Colonel Harwood had not endured himself much to the IAF. When he diverted into Tehran on our way into the country because he couldn't refuel, he took to berating the Iranian maintenance folks there, trying to get them to gas him up quickly so as to make it to Shiraz before dark. They didn't have the right fuel (JP-8) immediately available and couldn't get it there until the next morning. He then insisted they bring him a staff car and take him to make a "courtesy call" on the base commander. This was Tehran International Airport. There was no base commander. The colonel and his three mates were forced to sack out in the small military base operations building until morning, arriving in Shiraz with a pissed off colonel the next day. He managed to vent his spleen on General Ranjahni when they first met, and I don't think they ever met again until just before we departed for home.

The evening was amazing. General Ranjahni's wife was a beautiful and gracious hostess and a doting grandmother. Jani had brought his wife who had been Miss Iran six years ago, just before she and Jani got married. The women took the grandkids to one of the numerous rooms in the "chalet" while General Ranjahni and his son treated us to Cuban cigars and "The Balvenie 14," 14 year aged single malt. We had a good discussion, all initiated by the general about the current situation in Iran. He was a loyal Shah supporter, as it turned out so were almost all of the IAF officers. He had no time for the religious zealots and the rabble rousing students. He was concerned however, about the Shah's health and the apparent climate change of rebellion. It appeared that several senior army officers were sympathetic to the Muslim movement, and the general forecast trouble coming sooner rather than later. He felt it all hinged on when or if the Shah would return.

General Ranjahni told us a great story though. It seems he was dual qualified in the F-4 and the F-14. I think he also flew the A-4 and probably every other aircraft in the IAF inventory. Anyway, when the U.S. sold the Iranians the F-14, we also put several of their pilots and Weapons Systems Officers through training in Pensacola and Coronado Naval Air Stations. General Ranjahni was in one of the last classes just a few months back. He was at Coronado when a Hollywood crew rolled onto the base and set up to film a new movie - "Top Gun," starring Tom Cruise. The General and some of his classmates were actually extras in one of the scenes where Maverick and his buddies launch off on Cruise's quest to woo Kelly McGinnis with the song "You've Lost that Lovin' Feeling." The General asked me if I ever tried that line and had it worked. Since the movie had been delayed and hadn't come out yet, he had to describe the scene to us. I smiled and simply pled the Fifth to the question. Later, after I did see the movie when I was back in the States, I did try the line on some cute secretary at the Langley AFB Officer's Club one Friday night. I managed to get my face slapped and a hardy laugh from my friends.

There was another scene in the movie the General liked as well. It was the one where Maverick and Goose were being chased by one of the instructor pilots and Maverick pulls off some "never seen before" maneuver to turn the tables on the adversary. I guess General Ranjahni never forgot that scene and actually tried it on one of his wingmen when he returned to Iran. He said it didn't work too well. After seeing the movie later, I realized that it was pretty much a Hollywood hype maneuver. Maverick simply pulled the power to idle, extended the speed brakes, and pulled straight up into the vertical, hoping that the adversary would overshoot. The Tomcat has retractable wings, and the only way for the maneuver to even have a chance was to extend the wings at the same time, and there were airspeed limits to do that. I guess when the General tried it, he tried extending the wings at high airspeed and severely over Gd the jet.

CHAPTER TEN

FIGHTER PILOT

General Ranjahni was definitely a fighter pilot in every sense of the term. He was a very good pilot and as a leader, revered by his men. He had real credibility. That brings to mind what the term "fighter pilot" means, at least to me.

In my view "fighter pilot" isn't just a pilot who flies fighter type aircraft. In fact, I believe a person can have the same innate qualities of a fighter pilot without even flying airplanes. To me a fighter pilot is a person, male or female, who has the following traits (I'll call them a "he" here, but it can and does apply to many women as well):

1. He is very good at his job.
2. He has a bit of an ego, but not so much as to seem snobbish.
3. He is a bit of a daredevil, though not reckless or careless.
4. He has a good sense of humor.
5. As a leader he has great credibility.
6. He takes care of his people and they believe in him.

7. If he is in the military, he is good at following orders, but also is not averse at throwing the Bull Shit flag when he disagrees with his superiors.

There obviously can be a problem with that last one, and I'll be the first to admit that I've probably over-stepped the boundaries there a time or two. In fact, some of the best fighter pilots I know probably over-stepped their boundaries too often, and as a result their careers were short lived. A good example is General Robin Olds. He was an Ace with over five kills in the air spread over three wars. In fact, including WWII, Korea and Vietnam he had eleven kills. He was also a leader revered by his men. He partied hard, too hard for own sake. He bent the rules when it suited him, but almost always when he was right. His propensity to call a spade a spade and to do his own thing led to his being "retired on active duty." Because of his hero status as an Ace he was promoted to general officer, but then his superiors put him out to pasture by shipping him around the country giving speeches. Another military man who fits the definition of "fighter pilot" in much the same way was General George Patton. He pissed off his superiors and grounded him from the war at the end. He didn't fly, but he was a real "fighter pilot."

Rhino was a "fighter pilot" in every sense of the term to me. He was the best Weapons Systems Officer I ever flew with, and in fact, he could fly the jet almost as good as I could. Notice I said "almost." That's another trait of a real fighter pilot - he believes he is the best at what he does and takes every opportunity he can to prove it. Anyway, Rhino actually proved his flying skills to me often. I let him fly a bit on almost every sortie. In one occasion I came down with a killer of a sinus block as we were descending for landing. I was in serious pain and I gave Rhino the stick to land. I was monitoring the controls the best I could in my condition, but he made a firm, but safe landing. There were a few others of our WSOs who fit the bill as "fighter pilot" as well.

Other than Patton, these were all at least fliers, but as I said, I think the term "fighter pilot" is a state of mind, and it can apply to lots of folks, no matter what they do. Later in my career I was the Deputy for Operations of an F-16 wing back at Hahn Air Base. My best friend and cohort there was Jim McIntosh, the Chief of Maintenance. Often in the flying business operators and maintainers butt heads and work in an adversarial world. But Jim was a great leader of his troops, extremely credible, and we got along great. He believed that the mission came first and he would do everything he could to provide the operators with ready jets to fly. At the same time though, if we were pushing too hard and his troops needed a break, he would not hesitate to get in my face and say so.

After my Air Force career I had a job as the General Manager of a water utility in Colorado. I had a Superintendent of Operations who I consider a real "fighter pilot." He was the first one own in the ditch with his guys when we had a water main break. He worked his guys hard, but he took care of them as well. Again the word - "credibility."

In the water job I had occasion to work with lawyers, engineers, and politicians. I have to say I never met a politician I would call a "fighter pilot," but hopefully there are a few out there. I don't normally relish working with lawyers much either, but we had a water lawyer for our district who I consider a real go getter and a "fighter pilot." She was also a woman. She was so good at her job that the Colorado State Engineer was actually afraid to go up against her in court. As a result, we won a huge case against the State that saved us and our customers millions of dollars in water supply.

So, as far as I'm concerned a "fighter pilot" doesn't necessarily fly fighters. In fact, I know plenty of pilots who fly fighters who I wouldn't put in the same category. Several were with us on the mission to Iran. Our Squadron Commander, Lt. Col. Watson was a fighter pilot's fighter pilot. He was a great leader, an excellent stick, and he took care of his men. Later in my career I tried to emulate Colonel Watson when I took the helm of a squadron. At the same time we had Colonel Harwood, the Vice Wing Commander who couldn't refuel. He never fit the definition in my book, and I don't think he commanded much respect amongst the guys.

Enough pontificating on the egotistic, in your face, daredevil to dangerous, always questioning fighter pilot. Let's get back to Iran.

CHAPTER ELEVEN

THE FAIRER SEX

The women of Iran, or at least those in Shiraz, were a diverse mix of traditional Muslim and westernized modern ladies and girls. There were a few hard core Muslim women clad in their long robes and burkas, but for the most part they were in Tehran where all the turmoil was. The women weren't all as gorgeous as Jani's wife, or as classy and sophisticated as Jani's mother. But those that got out and about were inviting and enticing to a bunch of horny fighter pilots who had been on the road for over a month. They would often come into the hotel bar in groups of 3-5 all friendly and flirty …. to a point. The Sabers had been well briefed on customs and the instructions were basically to not get involved. As time went on that became more and more difficult. It seemed the same group of about a dozen girls came into the bar every Friday and Saturday night in threes and fours, and the same group of my squadron mates were there to entertain them with song and dance. Most of the girls spoke very good english and liked to practice it on the drooling American boys.

We had one or two follow up "chats" as a group from Colonel Watson. He didn't go on any of the "sweeps" of Shiraz's night life, but he did live in the same hotel as the rest of us and he could see what was going on in the bar. For the most part, he didn't have to worry. The same group of "players" that came in together each week always left together as well, much to the chagrin of one or two young Sabers who had thought they had died and gone to heaven.

There was one young lady however who stood out from the others. She was tall and drop dead gorgeous. She dressed impeccably and she was always alone. At least it started off that way. One of our young captain's was quick on the draw the first night she graced us with her presence at the hotel bar. He approached and she invited him to join her, but it was obvious he wasn't her type. At least it was obvious to the rest of us - not so much to him. She let him buy her drinks all night and she would dance with him or with one of the other guys who would butt in, but after a while she always got bored and left. This went on for a couple weeks and our intrepid captain finally got the signals and backed off. One Friday night the week we started winding things down, our young stud left her alone when she came into the bar. A couple of the other guys thought about trying their luck, but before they could make a move, she got up and bringing her drink with her, walked up to the bar and sat down next to one of the squadron new guys, Tom Luck. Tom was a lieutenant, and a loner. He had only joined the squadron a few days before our deployment, and because he was still in training, he didn't get to fly much in our integrated flying with the IAF. We managed to add on a few sorties here and there and Tom was at least able to keep flying enough to maintain landing currency. Tom was a good athlete though. He had played defensive end for Bear Bryant at Alabama, and was their backup kicker. Consequently, he was a good addition to our soccer team.

But Tom Luck was a loner. He was difficult to get to know and though most of us tried, it became obvious he just wanted to sit at the bar, nurse a couple drinks for an hour or so, and then turn in for the night. He seldom went with us on any of the sweeps or trips to other restaurants. But when Raiza Shamani came up and sat down beside him, he brightened up. They had a deep and long conversation - at least that's the way it seemed to us. Whenever any of us joined them to say hello, or to just be cordial, they both clammed up and just sat there. Finally, at about 11 PM, they got up from the bar, Tom paid the tab, and he walked Raiza out and put her in a cab ..... with half the squadron several feet in trail, trying to see what was going to happen next. When the taxi drove off Tom turned to go back in the hotel, spotted his drooling squadron mates, just shook his head, and retired to his room. The guys were disappointed.

The next night Tom and Raiza met again at the bar. They moved to a small table towards the rear of the room and continued their conversation, both of them looking at the other like star struck teenagers. They danced a few times - always to slow songs and in close and intimate. Actually Tom was an excellent dancer, and it was obvious that Raiza had some training. When they took to the dance floor, everyone else parted and gave them room to move as one around the floor, oblivious to anyone looking on. At about 10 PM Tom and Raiza slipped out almost unnoticed. This time he got in the taxi with her and they were gone.

Tom didn't make the bus the next morning, even though it was one of the days he was supposed to fly. His flight commander Don Kathcart covered for him, claiming Tom was feeling poorly and the flight was cancelled. Don and I had flown the morning shift and took the noon bus back to the hotel to check on Tom. He wasn't in his room and we convinced the maid to let us in to be sure he was okay. It was obvious he hadn't been there since yesterday. His bed hadn't been slept in and his boots and flight suit were where he'd obviously left them yesterday after flying. We didn't panic, but we decided that if he didn't show up in the restaurant or the bar tonight we needed to let Colonel Watson know what was going on, or at least what we knew.

Tom did not show that evening. Don and I waited until 9 PM and then went and knocked on Watson's door. Needless to say the Boss was none too pleased with us. Someone had lied this morning about Tom being sick and now it seems we have a U.S. Air Force lieutenant AWOL in Iran. None of us knew what to do, but I suggested I'd call Jani Ranjahni to see if he could help. "Yeah, I guess so," Colonel Watson bellowed, "but try to keep his father out of it. In the meantime, I guess I'd better go and enlighten Colonel Harwood so that he doesn't get blindsided on this."

Watson went off to the Vice Commander's suite and Don rounded up a bunch of guys to go and cruise the bars and restaurants that we frequented to see if Tom was anywhere to be found. I called Jani.

"Is she tall, with deep blue eyes and a very nice body?" Jani asked, as if he might know the girl.

"Yeah," I said. "I think her name is Raiza."

"It is. Raiza Shamani." He said. "This could be a real problem."

Jani went on to explain. Raiza Shamani was the daughter of a very high up government official in Iran who has a home in Shiraz. His 20 year old daughter lives in the home here while her father and mother are in their home in Tehran. She basically has no adult supervision and she is known for her escapades with international playboys. Evidently she also likes fighter pilots.

"A year ago she latched on to one of our squadron pilots who happens to be married, and they had a torrid affair that lasted for a couple of months." Jani explained. "The pilot's wife found out about it and word got around to Raiza's father in Tehran. Unfortunately he heard about it through the newspaper and was severely chastised and shamed. He came down hard on my father, and the pilot was reduced in rank to private and shipped off to a remote Air Force station in our mountains manning a radar sight. Raiza'a hand was slapped, but that was about it. Since then she's been spotted in many hotels and bars, and she's tried to hit on a few of my squadron mates. But my father made it very plain that Raiza Shamani was 'off limits' and as far as I know, she has not scored again. I suppose that's not the case now."

"Cheesh Jani. Anyway we can find her?" I asked.

"Hang on. My father is calling me on our home phone." Jani responded. When he came back up on the line, the news was not good.

It seems that Tom Luck and Raiza Shamani had been shacked up in her father's Shiraz mansion for the last 24 hours. Unfortunately for them, her father had installed closed circuit TV and a very loyal house servant who contacted his master when he viewed what can only be described as a "porn flick" starring Raiza and a big American who looked like a Hollywood type. Tom Luck's luck had run out. Daddy Shamani came roaring into town, though preceded by a squad of goons looking like Bruce Lee in black outfits, and masks. They took Tom out of the bedroom and worked him over to the point of unconsciousness with cuts and bruises all over his body. Especially violated were his privates. His manhood was beaten, bruised, and burned with cigarettes, and he was lucky they were not severed from his body.

After Raiza's father had abused Tom himself with what can only be described as an anal "dildo," he had him dumped at the front gate of the Air Base in Shiraz, simultaneously calling General Ranjahni to tell him where to find the infidel, among some other rants, raves and threats. The general had Luck picked up and delivered to the base hospital and called both Jani and Colonel Watson to meet him in the hospital room within the hour. Jani let me know the plan and I caught Colonel Watson leaving the hotel and begged for a ride. I had luck convincing him that I may be of value in what was to come next because of my relationship with Jani and his father. The Boss was fuming, but he saw through his furor and agreed.

What was to come next wasn't pretty, but we were lucky in one aspect. The Air Force had sent a C-9 "Nightingale" medic aircraft into Shiraz to pick up two of our enlisted maintenance folks who had come down with some sort of bug that was contagious and not within the capabilities of our medics' nor our hosts' to treat. In addition, the U.S. Embassy in Tehran had two staffers with similar symptoms that they had sent down to Shiraz by ambulance, and the jet was about to leave for Landstuhl Army Hospital in Germany. Colonel Watson was able to convince the C-9 pilot to delay and we went about springing Luck out of the hospital to the flight line. We simply dressed him in a hospital gown and when he was able to get out of bed we put him in a wheel chair and snuck him out a rear exit of the facility. Watson was waiting there with his assigned staff car and he delivered the lieutenant to the waiting flying ambulance.

General Ranjahni was pissed when he found out what had happened, but he realized that if Tom Luck was still in Iranian hands, Raiza's father would have a field day with him, bringing trumped up charges of rape and abuse with an Iranian girl. General Ranjahni knew of Raiza's escapades and he didn't want to see her lover castrated. At the same time though, Raiza's father was a powerful man, and when he found out what had happened, he came down hard on the general. He was black listed from the promotion list and it was obvious that Ranjahni's career was about to come to an end

CHAPTER TWELVE

FISHING TRIP

The next weekend Jani called me and said he wanted to return the favor for the times that I took him out fishing in Del Rio. He invited Rhino and I to go on a deep sea trip in the Persian Gulf. I thought it was a great opportunity, but Colonel Watson was not real keen on the idea. He worried about us straying too far from the ranch, especially since the incident with Tom. As it turned out however, Jani had an ulterior motive for the invitation and his father called Harwood and Watson to encourage them to let us go. We thought that a bit odd, but no one wanted to embarrass the U.S. or our hosts by turning them down. In many countries of the Muslim world, returning a favor is almost mandatory and Jani was simply following custom. We thought.

Apparently two days prior an American missionary had been captured in the town of Bushehr, about 100 miles southwest of Shiraz. He had been spreading bibles around and preaching the Christian gospel to the locals. That kind of thing always pisses off folks of different beliefs, and especially their masters who saw this as a way to achieve a major goal in their plot to overthrow the

Shah. The young man, Will Robertson, was thrown into a local jail in Bushehr and was accused of espionage by those opposing the Iranian regime. It became obvious that the regime was losing their battle to stay in power. When asked about the incident by our government they simply said they had no information to share

Logically the incident made it back to Washington, reported by Al Jaseera, a radical, Muslim slanted news organization. Footage of his capture showed Robertson with high tech camera and video equipment, several guns, and maps of local military bases - even the Air Base at Shiraz. Close ups of the missionary showed he had been beaten and roughed up considerably. A statement allegedly released by him admitted that he was working for the CIA.

We had not heard of the incident yet in Shiraz. At least it hadn't gotten down to the captain level yet. I suppose Colonel Harwood had been briefed in on one of his calls back to the home base. Jani was definitely read in on the whole thing and our fishing trip became very interesting.

Jani picked Rhino and I up at the hotel at 7 AM and we drove out to the base to a waiting helicopter. Already on board were four of the roughest looking characters I had ever seen. We were all in civilian clothes, but these guys were obviously some kind of special forces operators - high and tight haircuts, bulging muscles, and they had other bulges under their clothing that indicated they were all heavily armed. Jani explained that they were his "bodyguards" - that the area we were headed to had recently seen some skirmishes with bandits, and his father wanted to be sure we would all be safe. Rhino and I looked at each other with arched eyebrows.

The chopper deposited us in a parking lot next to a marina in the port of Bushehr. There were several deep sea fishing rigs, a few sailboats, and one gorgeous luxury yacht, about 85 feet in length. She bared the name "Persian Princess." That was to be our fishing vessel for the day. We actually did do some fishing off the stern and sides of the boat. I caught a couple nice red snappers and Rhino caught a big yellow fin tuna. The boat had a chef among its crew of six, and he fixed the fish up for us with all the trimmings for lunch. Jani even brought out a cooler of beer for us to enjoy. Would you believe it - Lone Star longnecks? I asked Jani how he managed to get Lone Star beer delivered to the other side of the world from Texas. He never did really answer.

Jani cut the fishing trip short about 1 PM and we headed back to port. On the way he sat down beside us and asked if we had heard about the American missionary who was in custody for espionage in Bushehr.

"No," I reacted. "What's that all about?"

"He was supposedly caught taking photos of the navy base in Bushehr and he had photos of Shiraz and other military installations as well." Jani related. "I'm told he has confessed to working for the CIA."

I knew this kind of thing happened often. Americans abroad apprehended doing suspicious activities and held in prisons in Russia, South America, other locations where the host country is not exactly our ally. Whether they were guilty or not, many of them were still rotting in foreign jails because of our policy of not dealing with "terrorists." But I hadn't heard of the problem in Iran and I was curious why Jani was telling us all this, so I asked him.

"The Ayatollahs are holding the man for ransom to force the United States to turn the Shah over to them in exchange. My father and most Iranians currently in power do not want anything to happen to the Shah. He is currently in France but he has asked your government for asylum so that he can have his cancer treated. The Ayatollahs believe that this one missionary is worth the trade for the Shah."

"My father is hoping you can help by visiting the missionary and reporting back to your government his innocence, and then maybe coming to rescue him."

"Whoa! Jani. This is way above my pay grade!" I said. "I guess we can go see him, but I sure can't guarantee we could even get an audience with those in our government who would make a difference."

"I understand." He said, "And my father does as well. Perhaps you can come up with some other plan."

I had no idea what that meant and once again I looked at Rhino. We both simply shrugged our shoulders.

The "prison" in Bushehr was more like a pig sty surrounded by barbed wire. We were escorted in by a couple of rough looking guards who seemed to know who Jani was and why he might be here. Will Robertson was alive, but in terrible shape. He had been beaten, whipped and drugged up. He hardly even acknowledged we were there. It really pissed me off to see a fellow American treated this way.

"Jani, who did this to him and why?" I demanded.

"All I can tell you it wasn't these guards. I don't know specifically who beat on him, but they obviously wanted him to confess to whatever it is they suspect he did." Jani replied. Then he dropped the bomb on us.

"These guards are loyal to my father and they would not interfere if there was an attempt to rescue the prisoner." He left it at that and looked at us with inquisitive eyes.

"What are you saying Jani?" I asked. "Do you expect us to break him out of here? That's not exactly the kind of business we're in. We fly jets. We're not CIA types or even special ops."

"No, no." Jani said. "I don't expect you to do it, but you can take information back to your countrymen who do have that kind of capability and mission." Then he spoke to one of the guards who produced a file with a layout of the prison complex, and even the guard rotation schedule. He gave it to Jani who looked it over and handed it to me.

"These guards aren't on duty all of the time, so this schedule shows when they are. The others won't be quite as receptive to a break out." He paused. "I think we should leave now."

We left the prison and were driven to a local school yard where the helicopter was waiting, engines running and ready to go. Jani never spoke a word all the way back to Shiraz. I didn't either. I was trying to think about what exactly he, or probably his father, expected us to do. My mind came up with all kinds of clandestine ideas, most of which I've read about in spy novels. I decided I needed to go directly to the boss and let him and Colonel Harwood in on the real purpose of our "fishing trip."

CHAPTER THIRTEEN

WASHINGTON D.C.

I went directly to Colonel Watson when we got back to the squadron. I told him the story and suggested we HAD to do something about that poor kid in the jail.

"Whoa. Slow down Mitchell." the boss said. "I know you're pissed. Hell, so am I, but this is way out of our league and I don't want you getting more involved than you already are. In fact, come with me. Let's go talk to Colonel Harwood about this. He might have some questions."

We went to the Vice Commander's office that he had set up in the squadron complex and I told him the story. Harwood went on a rant.

"Jesus Christ Watson. Can't you keep these guys on a leash." Harwood dumped on the boss. "First this Lieutenant who couldn't keep his dick in his pants, and now you got guys trying to drum up an international incident. In fact, from what I've heard, the issue with Lt. Luck already is an international incident."

"Sir, I understand." Watson came back. "But it is very obvious that General Ranjahni and his son are giving us the opportunity to spring an American in a shit hole of a jail. I think we need to at least run it up the flagpole. I've instructed Mitchell here to stay out of it. These guys are fighter pilots, not special operators looking to be heroes." He looked at me when he added that last statement and I could feel his stare going right through me.

"All Right. I'll contact USAFE. Mitchell stick around though. I'd bet the brass will want to talk to you about specifics." Harwood said.

"Yes sir. I understand and I have these plans and guard schedules that Jani gave me. They will probably be of some use." I responded.

In Washington it was Monday morning. A hastily called meeting of the brass and the national security team had been requested by the Chairman of the Joint Chiefs, Admiral Lester Miller. Colonel Harwood had contacted the USAFE Commander in Chief General Walter Bong, who in turned passed on the information to the Chief of Staff of the Air Force, General Ron Furman. On up the chain it went.

Present in the Situation Room of the White House were the President, the Chairman, CSAF, CIA Director Richard Durkee, Assistant Secretary of Defense, Madeline Dunlap, the National Security Director Mike Nash, Secretary of State Tim Conlin, and the White House Chief of Staff J. Bobby Taggart. The Vice President, Joseph Michaels and SECDEF Lawrence Malloy were both out of the city.

President Carver had swept into office behind the Watergate affair and he was basically out of his element when dealing with foreign affairs. He had been, and still was a peanut farmer in southern Virginia, rose in politics in that state to Lt. Governor, and then moved up when the governor was caught in a relationship with one of his aides. Carver was not a dummy, he just sometimes came across that way. Fortunately he had surrounded himself with some pretty good folks with a little experience. There were some "strap hangers" as well, like Chief of Staff J. Bobby Taggart, but for the most part sanity prevailed, though often with too much partisan politics.

"So what's going on fellas?" The President said, looking first at the Chairman of the JCS.

"Sir, I believe you were briefed on the missionary the Iranians have in custody. As you know, the revolutionaries in Tehran want us to turn the Shah over to them and they are holding this missionary hostage for an exchange. We may have an alternative." The Chairman said.

"We don't even have the Shah," Carver responded. "I talked to him this morning and he desperately wants us to grant him asylum so he can get his cancer treatments. I told him we would consider it and I'm inclined to let him come. He's been a good friend."

Mr. President, that might be a big mistake." It was Tim Conlin, Secretary of State. "The situation in Iran is in a turmoil right now. The government of the Shah remains but hanging by a shoestring. The Ayatollahs have stirred up a hornets' nest of radicals who are within days of launching a coup. In fact, I am concerned for our folks at the embassy. I've told the ambassador to bring everyone into the embassy compound, be ready to evacuate, and to send as many dependents home as he can."

"I understand and I guess I agree. Bobby tells me this missionary's parents have been in contact through Congressman Davis and they are demanding we do something." The President indicated to J. Bobby Taggart, his White House Chief of Staff.

"Yes sir. Congressman Wade Davis of Utah contacted me and I guess the kid's parents are up in arms, and want us to pay ransom or whatever will work to get the kid released." Taggart responded.

"So what's new Admiral?" The President asked

Admiral Miller, General Furman, and Richard Durkee briefed the group on the missionary's status and the strange proposal evidently brought forth by a General Ranjahni of the Iranian Air Force. There was a lot of skepticism, especially on the President's part.

"So, what was this kid really doing there?" The President asked, looking directly at Durkee. "Was he working for you?"

Durkee tap danced. "Sir I have no direct knowledge of his activities. It is most likely his charges were trumped up."

"No direct knowledge? Most likely?" It was Taggart that rolled in on the CIA Chief. The two had words before and there was no love lost either direction. "Have they caught one of your spies red handed Durkee?"

The Director turned as red as a beet. "Mr. Taggart let me remind you that there parts of the way this government works that don't involve you and I'll be damned if I'm going to defend our covert operations to you."

"Ah, so he is part of your 'covert' operations." Taggart came back.

The Chairman jumped in. "Mr. President I think we need to move on and discuss the opportunity we may have at hand. Whether this man is a CIA operative or a real missionary, shouldn't matter. He is a true blue American who apparently has been beaten and roughed up, and I believe we should try and get him out."

"So Admiral, are you saying we should trade him for the Shah?" The President asked.

"No sir. We believe there is another way."

The staff briefed the President on the situation and evidently discussed our trip to Bushehr and the apparent carrot being dangled by General Ranjahni. They brought General Bong into the meeting by phone from his headquarters in Germany.

"General, how credible do you think this captain of yours and his Iranian friends are?" The President asked Bong.

"Sir, Captain Mitchell is one of our F-4 pilots based out of Hahn Air Base here in Germany. He was the instructor pilot for the Iranian captain when he went through our pilot training in Texas. The two struck up a rapport, and the Iranian's father is the two star commander of the base at Shiraz. In fact, Captain Mitchell flew with the general on one training mission and Mitchell and his squadron commander spent a nice social evening with their hosts. They seem to believe what the Iranians are offering is credible, especially in light of recent circumstances." General Bong realized immediately that bringing up the 'recent circumstances' might be a bad move.

"What recent circumstances General?" Taggart asked.

Bong hesitated a minute, but then went ahead, "Apparently General Ranjahni has fallen out of graces in Tehran, especially with a senior government official who apparently has it in for him." He went on to explain the situation with Lt. Tom Luck and Raiza Shamani, and her father.

"The general has basically been sidelined and is destined for demotion or worse." Bong went on. "We think he might be looking for a way out himself, but at the very least he doesn't seem to want to go out quietly. The documentation and plans his son provided Captain Mitchell could certainly provide means for the general to go out with a bang."

"So let me get this straight General." It was Taggart again. "One of your lieutenants couldn't keep his pecker in its holster and you had to smuggle him out of the country?"

"Mr. President, I submit that this 'interrogation' of General Bong is highly inappropriate, as is Mr. Taggart's language with a lady in the room." General Furman jumped in to the rescue.

"Don't worry about me General." Assistant SECDEF Madeline Dunlap chimed in. "I've heard a lot worse, but I do agree we don't need to be discussing the sexual prowess of our fighter pilots, but should concentrate on the question at hand. Should we make an attempt to rescue this American in an Iranian pig sty?"

"Well put Ms. Dunlap and thank you." The President motioned for Taggart to back off. "So what you're proposing Admiral is that we trust this Iranian general and using information provided by his son, we go in and rescue our American missionary - or whatever he is?" The President shifted back to the Chairman.

"Yes sir. I am."

CHAPTER FOURTEEN

GRADUATION

I didn't hear anything more about the missionary other than what we got on the news. The U.S. government was not about to deal a trade of the Shah of Iran for an American spy. At least that's the way Al Jazeera portrayed everything. I kept my nose to the grind flyin' and fightin,' or at least pretending to fight. The flying in Shiraz had gone very well. The IAF squadron progressed well in the tactical environment and the Tenth aircrews had the opportunity to train with munitions they might never see again, and in an environment that some of them would relate to later on in their careers. With about ten days to go in the deployment, a week after the Tom Luck incident and a couple days after our trip to Bushehr, there was a two day "graduation" exercise that involved Iranian Air Force, Army and Navy forces. It was a two pronged attack scenario where the F-4s acted as aggressor forces attacking an army mechanized division near Bushehr, and a mass attack on the Iranian naval fleet just off the coast due south of Shiraz in the Persian Gulf. The army was "protected" by many of the missile and artillery emitter sights represented on their electronic range. The emitters had been brought down and strategically positioned around Bushehr. The navy was protected by F-14s with the Phoenix missile, as well as some older A-4s in their inventory. This was all scheduled with simulated weapons - no real bombs or missiles.

The first day was conducted like our first day flying in country. IAF flight leaders with Sabers flying numbers three and four. Half of us attacked the army in Bushehr, the other half launched against the navy. They had two large cruisers and four destroyers, positioned about 20 miles off shore. There were gunboats running around as well, and we were told they had two submarines out there too. Needless to say we didn't see either of them. It was as if the IAF crews hadn't learned a thing when planning for the attacks. They did manage to brief and fly tactical formations, but at medium altitudes of 5000 to 10,000 feet - right in the heart of the envelope of the defending missiles and guns.

Another batch of "goodies" the U.S. had supplied Iran with was chaff. Chaff is bundles of aluminum that is loaded in a dispenser in the tail of the aircraft, often with flares as well. When activated by the pilot, the dispenser ejects the chaff, and hopefully any radar that is trying to track him will transfer its lock to the chaff. The flares are used similarly to divert incoming heat seeking missiles. We had not used them in the deployment so far, although we had brought it up during our missions on the electronic range. We sure could have used some chaff on this mission, especially at mid altitudes when they could see us coming and lock on before we got even close to our weapons parameters. The rules of engagement (ROE) for the exercise was heavily skewed toward the good guys, in this case the army and their defenses, and the Navy and the F-14s. All the Tomcat crews had to do was lock on to an incoming jet and simulate a shot, and they called it out on the radio as a "kill." If we were "killed" we had to leave the fight and return to Shiraz to land. On that first day only two four ships of attackers got through to the army forces, and everyone of the attackers against the navy were "killed" by Phoenix shots before they even broke the coast outbound. Basically we just bored holes in the sky.

The Phoenix, officially known as the AIM-54 air to air radar guided missile, was another "brilliant decision" our politicians made back when we considered Iran our friend. The missile was originally developed for use on the Air Force's FB-111, but by the time it was ready, the AF decided to go another direction with the Aardvark. So the only users of the Phoenix were the U.S. Navy and Iran on F-14 Tomcats. Since we had sold the F-14 to Iran, I guess it made sense to include the Phoenix in the sales package. The F-14 has a very powerful radar that can pick up targets 100 miles away, and lock on to shoot at about 60 miles. The big Phoenix missile actuates its own radar at about 11 miles from the target, and one F-14 can track up to 24 targets and launch up to 6 Phoenix missiles at once. Iran had lot better results with the missile than our Navy did. They claimed 62 kills in their war with Iraq. It wasn't until Desert Storm in the 1990s that our Navy used it, shooting three total Phoenix missiles at Iraqi aircraft, missing all three. Anyway, suffice it to say that the IAF could reliably claim a simulated "kill" on us before we could even see them on radar. Frustrating.

I was in the force that attacked the army, although I was "killed" early by a simulated surface to air missile (SAM). The next day I led one of the attacks on the navy. As soon as we hit the deck on that first day I had looked up Jani Ranjahni and rode him hard to spring lose some chaff for our mission the next day. Between he and Colonel Watson they were able to convince Jani's dad to authorize it, and all the jets (ours and theirs) were loaded with chaff. We held a quick academic session that afternoon on chaff and when to use it.

I led a twelve ship gorilla package on the navy. Our other twelve aircraft were led by Lt. Colonel Fracelli, our squadron operations officer. Each of us had six USAF and six IAF jets and crews. The rest of our squadron and theirs were led by Colonel Watson and Major Tony Gilford against the army. They basically did a pincer attack on the target area, coming in at low altitude from two directions. Only four of their 24 aircraft were "shot down." The low level masking and the use of chaff surprised and/or defeated the defenses, so the division of tanks and artillery were turned into simulated burned out hulks.

There is a large mesa between Shiraz and the coast. It is about 1000 feet in elevation, so I used it to our advantage on our attack of the navy. We stayed at low level after launch and followed the contour of the mesa east and south keeping the rocks between us and the navy. The F-14s were between the coast and the ships and although they probably suspected we would come in low, they weren't able to pick any of us up until about 50 miles out from our target when our mesa broke off to our west, leaving us exposed. From there on out to the coast Iran is basically a desert with some hills here and there. Our plan was for my "gorilla" to press straight for the ships once exposed by the loss of our cover. "Smooth" took his twelve ship due south to try an end around and attack from the southeast over the water. That at least served to split the F-14s up. I knew that the Tomcats would be able to "paint" us with their radars soon after we were exposed. However, by staying down on the deck, we were able to at least make it difficult for them. Their weapons systems officers didn't have much experience looking down into the ground clutter on their radars. After all, most of their "targets" in the past were cooperative IAF bozos at medium to high altitudes. We did get several Phoenix shots called at us. I think most of the time they were against some of the IAF pilots flying a little higher than we were, simply because they were not comfortable down in the rocks yet. I had briefed that if we were targeted (evidenced by our radar warning receivers), we would make a hard turn as two ships to put the Tomcat on the beam (wingtip) and pump out some chaff. If that broke the lock, we would turn back in and continue. If not, we would time out the simulated missile flight time, and if they still had us locked, we would follow the rules, break out of the formation, and go home as a "kill."

Because there were so many of us and coming at them from two directions, we only lost a total of eight attackers to the Phoenix - 6 IAF and two Sabers. The rest of us all made at least one defensive turn with chaff, and were able to turn back in and blow right through the F-14s. They never expected us to "survive" so they were sitting ducks as we simulated AIM-7 radar missile and AIM-9 heat seeker shots on them. Bosco and Boomer each even got some good gun camera film tracking Tomcats. After blowing through the air patrol I dove for the water and with at least six of us (all USAF) blew across the cruisers and destroyers ala Tom Cruise in Top Gun. The IAF guys in my flight did not participate in the "fly by." They just hung out in an orbit playing with the few A-4s that had not turned tail and run away. Even Jani, who was flying as my number three stayed out of the fray. I pulled off the swoop and ordered the gorilla to rejoin to some semblance of tactical formation as we climbed out to return to Shiraz. Fracelli's attack came about five minutes after ours, and although he didn't "shine his ass" afterwards trying to spill the cruiser captains' coffee, he did substantial simulated damage as well.

When we got back to base and debriefed the mission the F-14 guys and the navy were furious. They called in their complaints to the base and General Ranjahni got word of it post haste. He came down to the squadron and sat in on my debrief. We went over our gun camera films and listened to shot calls and radar warning responses, and I particularly highlighted the "kill" shots on the F-14s. The general smiled through all of that, but when he saw a couple of the ship attacks he wasn't smiling. I had conveniently turned my camera off for that pass, as had most of my guys, but there were two that had not. Both General Ranjahni and later Lt. Colonel Watson, frowned at seeing the superstructure of a big cruiser so close and personal. It seems Colonel Harwood was in the debriefing as well, although he had not flown on the mission. He was livid and he and Colonel Watson had a rather heated, one sided discussion. Suffice it to say, I got my ass chewed by our squadron commander, though admittedly with a bit of a smile while he chewed. I stayed away from Harwood for the rest of the deployment.

CHAPTER FIFTEEN

IN THE MEANTIME

Unbeknownst to us, and apparently to the Iranians, an American team of Navy Underwater Demolition experts were transported to a position outside the port of Bushehr the night of the first day of our exercise. They were inserted as close as possible by the attack submarine USS Virginia and launched off in a rubber Zodiac boat with a very quiet electric engine.

The UDT personnel are the precursors to later day SEAL teams. It wasn't until 1983 that the SEALS stood up their own mission, but we're talking about the same folks, with the same training. This team was lead by Master Chief Ryun Moore. He and his team of three others were the elite in their little realm. They were based out of Fort Pierce, Florida, but they weren't home much. The UD Teams had transformed from straight underwater demolition and mine warfare to selective special operations that involved insertion and/or extraction by sea. They had been working with the CIA on several operations, from the rescue of intelligence operators to the destruction of high valued yet clandestine targets.

Moore's particular team had just returned from a gun running intercept mission off the Cuban coast.

The team had been flown from Jacksonville, Florida Naval Air Station to Incirlik Air Base in Turkey. There they boarded an Air Force C-130, and in the dark of night took off to rendezvous with the USS Virginia in the Persian Gulf. They parachuted off the big Hercules into a dark night of rough seas, and fortunately the C-130 pilot was right on target. Actually, I'm sure it was probably the navigator's show. Within minutes of the last man splashing down, the conning tower of the Virginia emerged from below. It took less than ten minutes for the UD Team to climb aboard and be ushered below. After a quick meal and a little rest they adjourned to a table in the Captain's quarters where they received their final briefing.

The Zodiac boats were low profile, and the electric engine made them very quiet. In fact, if there is any surf noise at all, no one near the landing zone could hear them coming. They beached in a small secluded cove and pulled the boat up on shore and covered it with bushes. One of the guys used a branch to sweep the tracks off the sand, just like they do in cowboy movies. Then, having memorized the layout of the town of Bushehr that they were provided from U-2 reconnaissance footage, they set off for the back alleys that led to the infamous prison.

Since the so called "friendly" guards had no idea when or even if there would be a break out attempt, the UDT had to approach them in complete stealth and surprise them. That was easier than it should have been. At least one of the guards had been drinking and was almost falling down drunk. Master Chief Moore halted their progression when they came up on the guard. He was leaning against a corner of the building taking a piss. Moore dispatched one of his guys to subdue the guard, and the operator decided to let him finish his watering the local gutter, if for no other reason than to avoid being sprayed by urine when he took the guard out. Bozo stuffed himself back into his pants and was about to turn around when he was caught in a choke hold that he couldn't break. In fact, he couldn't even breathe and he passed out in a few seconds. The operator laid the Iranian down quietly and they used zip ties to basically hogtie him, and stuffed a rag in his mouth. Now to find the other guard.

Moore thought it a bit odd that there would only be two guards on duty for such an apparently high value prisoner. But evidently the higher ups in the Iranian rebellion thought differently. They figured that no one would think to look for a prisoner in such a hell hole of a pig sty jailhouse as that in the little town of Bushehr. They of course had not reckoned on Jani Ranjahni and his father having the information they did. At any rate, the second guard was inside the building sitting (or dozing off) at a desk in an outer room of the two room building. Remember how the sheriff's office of the jail in Gunsmoke or any of the Duke's movies always had a desk, a rack of rifles, a couple of chairs, and probably a spittoon? Well, there you have it. "Festus" was nodding off at the desk while "Mr. Dillon" must have been over at the Longbranch, hitting on Miss Kitty. The only difference here was they didn't even have a rack of rifles. The guard had a rifle leaning against his chair, but that was it. Once again it was easy to subdue the guard, and this time they kept him awake, though gagged, so they could let him understand that this was the breakout they had been expecting.

There was one other difference between this jail and the one Matt Dillon and Festus manned. This place really was a slophouse. It was basically a sewer trough enclosed in chain link and barbed wire. Will Robertson was laying against one wall with human excrement, garbage, rats, and even some big ass spiders all around him. He was conscious, but barely. Moore was able to arouse him and get him to his feet, though it took two of his team mates to keep the man up. The UDT dragged Robertson out, and on the way Moore made sure the guard was awake when he shoved a hundred dollar bill in his pocket. That was probably not a great idea in case the Mullah muckety mucks interrogated their guards and found out that an American team had come and spirited off with their prize American spy. It actually was a lot better that the team got in, got their man, and got gone without anyone of substance knowing it.

The team made it back to their getaway boat and out to sea without any resistance. They motored out about two miles and the Virginia surfaced right beside them as quiet as a mouse. In fact, the surprise of the conning tower surfacing within 20 feet of the Zodiac was probably the most excited the team got all night. Once aboard, Robertson went to the sick bay, and the Virginia submerged and high tailed it to Bahrain. Mission accomplished.

CHAPTER SIXTEEN

TIME TO GO

All hell broke loose the next day. The Mullahs and Ayatollahs were on fire. The Shah had contacted the U.S. for permission to come into the country for his cancer treatments That fact was leaked to the press, and the rebels' trump card was missing. They had no idea what had happened to their prisoner, but they were sure that America was behind his disappearance. The two guards were severely chastised and about to be put to death, but from what Jani told me his father was able to save them and gave them a job with the same group of "bodyguards" that had accompanied us on the fishing trip. The Ayatollah was calling for "death to America," and the students at Tehran's largest university rioted and burned half the place down. The police were able to keep a semblance of order, but mainly by just standing by and letting things unfold. In addition, the issue with Tom Luck and Raiza Shamani had blossomed to a full blown international incident in the Iranian press. Colonel Harwood was summoned to General Ranjahni's office. Colonel Watson went along for moral support. The general basically ordered us to get out of town while we still could. He offered his communications center for our coordination with USAFE and the Pentagon. There was no discussion of the rescue mission. General Ranjahni obviously had an idea of what had happened, but he didn't know who in his staff he could trust, so he kept mum about the whole affair.

Colonel Watson immediately called the squadron and got Fracelli organizing our redeployment. It was December 9th and the best we thought we could do was to launch off on the 11th. We had a lot of gear to pack and tankers and airlift to coordinate. In the meantime, Watson and Harwood got on the horn to USAFE headquarters, back in Ramstein, Germany. Because of the late night activity before, the staff was mostly in attendance and Harwood was able to contact General Bong, and he in turn, contacted the four star Commander in Chief at the Pentagon. Things warmed up then. Within six hours, a C-141 Stratolifter that had been turning from a mission in Quatar and was due to return to the states, had been diverted into Shiraz. The maintainers and admin folks went about organizing, packing and loading the big jet for a departure the next day, December 10th. The big problem was we had three grounded F-4s for one reason or another. Two of them were relatively minor issues and the maintenance Officer in Charge (OIC) thought they could have them ready to go by launch time. The third however needed an engine change. It had taken a bird on recovery from the gaggle mission a few days ago and the engine was trashed. The hope was that we could "borrow" an engine from the Iranians, and the plan was to leave enough crew chiefs and a couple engine specialists at Shiraz, a total of 14 folks to change the engine and launch the fleet on time on the

11th. Everyone else was to get on the C-141 with all our gear and a few aircrew that would not be in the flight package on the 10th and get them out of Dodge, to Hahn. The 14 folks left behind would return via commercial airlines and tickets were purchased leaving directly from Shiraz to Dhahran, Saudi Arabia. They could connect there to just about anywhere in the world. A maintenance captain was put in charge of the small contingent.

Colonels Harwood and Watson worked on the engine repair issue all night and most of the next day. We thought the engine loan (really a "sale" for about ten times what the Pratt & Whitney engine was worth), was a done deal when on Sunday morning a contingent of the Iranian Army led by a general moved on base and basically put Major General Ranjahni under arrest. They also posted guards throughout the base, keeping a close eye on not only the Americans, but the IAF squadron crews as well. Our request for an engine was denied.

The launch on Sunday was scheduled for noon to meet a pair of tankers coming out of Incirlik Air Base in Turkey out over the Med as soon as we broke the coast outbound. With one good refueling we could make Hahn if the weather there was decent. If not, we would go into Aviano Air Base in northern Italy. From there we could just wait out the weather and one hop it into Hahn later. We went with five four ship formations and one three ship, leaving the wounded bird on the ramp. The other two maintenance problems were in the works and would make up two of the last three to launch.

Colonel Watson was to lead the first flight with Colonel Harwood on his wing. The other four flights of four were to be led by Smooth Fracelli, Tony Gilford, and two flight commanders, Larry "Clit" Katorian and Scotty "Beam me up" Perkins. I had the "honor" of going last with the three stragglers. I was to wait until all three were ready and go into Incirlik if I couldn't make it to the tanker on time. I had Rhino in the pit and two lieutenants on the wing - "Boomer" Huston and "Bosco." Since Boomer had completed his flight lead checkout program while we were there, all he needed was a flight lead check ride, so since I was a check pilot instructor, I set him up as the leader, and I flew as Number Three. Boomer was an outstanding stick - the best lieutenant I ever flew with and he had impressed everyone in the squadron. It was very rare for lieutenants to get checked out as four ship flight leads, but Boomer was a rare exception. The epitome of the term "fighter pilot." He had done well leading four ships with IAF crews as number three and four, even to the range and through refueling. He actually led one of the four ships in my twelve ship gaggle against the navy with an instructor on his wing. He did accompany us as we blew by the cruiser, but I took all the heat for that as the overall leader. Bosco was also a great fighter pilot and he too was in the flight lead check out program, just lacking a couple more upgrade flights.

At about 10 AM on Sunday, December 11, 1978 the radical Muslims, backed by thousands of students and a good portion of the Iranian army, overthrew the government in Tehran. They threw all of the Shah's underlings in jail, rioted in the streets, burning anything that smacked of the government and the Shah, and staged a huge protest in front of the American embassy. They shutdown the power to the embassy, and the state run TV station, and took over the control tower at Tehran International Airport. No flights were allowed in or out. We got the word in Shiraz and immediately scrambled to our jets. Well most of us did. Bosco's designated jet was not quite ready yet. It had an inertial navigation system problem and after working on it all night, the maintenance OIC had directed that the INS be changed out. They were in the process of pulling the unit out of the wounded bird with one engine when the shit hit the fan. I waited with my flight while everyone else stepped to fly. The flight plans were filed already, so I had Rhino and Fubar working with the locals to push up the takeoff times. They went ahead and filed six flight plans, betting on the come we would get off with the last three sometime soon.

The Sabers cranked up their steeds and were ready to go about 11 AM. One of the wingmen had a flight control problem, so he didn't taxi with the rest. He shut down and the maintenance guys worked like champs to try to get him back up. Colonel Watson decided to taxi all of them at once, and if necessary, take off as one gaggle, sorting out the spacing later. Because they were launching an hour early, they weren't sure they'd have a tanker up there to meet or not. I was working that angle. Evidently the folks who had taken over the airport in Tehran took over the air traffic control system as well. Flights that were inbound were ordered to turn around, leave Iranian airspace, and land someplace else. Flights that were outbound were instructed to sit tight. Because of that, Colonel Watson could not get a clearance for the flight. He pulled a fast one on the tower folks then. He requested a VFR (Visual Flight Rules) clearance to simply take off and fly around without flight following, as if they would simply be practicing traffic patterns. The civilians in the Shiraz tower were confused. They didn't need a clearance from air traffic control to authorize a VFR flight, and I guess they couldn't come up with a reason to deny the request. Nineteen Sabers took off as one big gorilla and climbed out heading northwest. It was a good thing the weather was perfect - very clear with only a few high clouds. If they would have had to request flight following to go into the weather, chances are they would have been denied. As it was, the Iranian air traffic control folks were screaming at them on the radio to come up on their frequencies, and the boss simply ignored them.

The flight control problem of the one wingman took too long so he taxied back in and was refueled while the issue was corrected. I now had a four ship to deal with. The problem was though that I was the only certified flight lead in the formation. I just kind of overlooked that issue and flew as number three, put the new wingman on my wing, and put Boomer out front.

I got in contact with Jani Ranjahni. His dad was under house arrest, but they had basically left him alone with his squadron. They were ordered to stay in their squadron building and not plan on any flying. The squadron had a mini command post with communications through the base command post and Jani was able to get me a phone line to call USAFE headquarters. I got in contact with the officer on duty and he patched me through to the USAFE Director of Operations. I told him the situation and requested he contact the tankers at Incirlik to scramble them early and to have Incirlik work with Turkish ATC to file flight plans for the gorilla that was inbound to Turkey. I also asked him to try and scare up an engine for our wounded bird and try to get it delivered to Shiraz.

Two hours later I had four jets ready to go. So at about 1:30 we stepped to our jets and cranked them up. Boomer had briefed a good mission, but I decided I would deal with the tower folks and give him the lead after we got airborne. I think he was relieved, and I'm pretty sure he was after he witnessed what we did to get airborne. We taxied out without contacting the ground control folks in the tower. I simply led us out to the runway. We had done all of the pre-takeoff checks in the chocks prior to taxiing, so when we got to the end of the runway, I looked right and left for traffic and rolled on. At that point I radioed the tower and simply announced "Shiraz Tower Saber 61 is taking the runway for VFR takeoff." There was a pregnant pause while we ran the engines up, then "Saber 61 negative. You are not cleared for takeoff. You are to abort and taxi back to your parking." I didn't even hesitate. I quickly told the flight we will make formation takeoffs and then faked radio problems "Shiraz Tow … Saa…61, you …broken… say…gain." I released the brakes, selected full afterburner and we were all airborne in about 30 seconds with the radio squawking loud and clear. Since it was a 13,000 foot runway, formation takeoffs even as heavy weight as we were turned out to be fine.

We climbed out towards Turkey and I gave the lead to Boomer. We turned our radios to the Air Traffic Control frequency and they called us several times. Boomer picked up on the idea though - we all obviously had radio problems. He also kicked us all out to a tactical box formation. I pretty much expected an F-14 or F-4 to come up to intercept us. We kept our heads on swivels, checking six. Sure enough, as we crossed into Turkey, their Air Traffic Control came up on the guard emergency frequency and broadcast "American F-4 flight crossing into Turkish airspace from the east, contact Turkey Center on frequency 320.9." We did so, and they gave us a clearance and IFF (Identification Friend or Foe) number to squawk. IFF is a system that highlights a radar "blip" and can tell the controller on the ground the call sign and altitude of the target they are tracking.

Unfortunately we missed the tankers. They had scrambled when they got the word from USAFE and made it to the refueling track in time for the Saber gorilla. That allowed the bulk of the squadron to go on into Hahn. But that was two and a half hours ago and the tankers had moved on. Boomer took us into Incirlik. As it turned out that was a good thing for another reason.

Back at Shiraz the army went ballistic. They corralled our maintenance guys and placed them under arrest in their tents, posting guards all around. The USAF captain in charge of the contingent produced the airline tickets they had, assuming that leaving Iran is what the Iranians wanted. Bad assumption. What the Iranians wanted were hostages, and now they had 14 Americans and one USAF F-4 to tout about on the news. They may have lost their "spy" missionary, but now they had something better. Even Jani and his squadron commander, nor his father, could do anything to help.

CHAPTER SEVENTEEN

WASHINGTON

CNN started broadcasting coverage of the turmoil in Tehran at about 6 AM East Coast Time. The takeover was a few hours old by then, but they decided no one would be up on a Sunday morning to care about a bunch of rag heads fighting amongst themselves. About 9 o'clock however, they showed coverage of an American fighter jet on the ramp in Shiraz with Iranian guards around it and guards around a tent city that had a big sign on it "Tenth TFS South." It was assumed there were Americans inside.

The National Security team had re-assembled in the White House. The President came in and motioned for the Chairman to proceed.

"Sir, I assume you are aware of the coup or takeover in Iran?" The admiral asked, not wanting to waste a lot of time with the build up.

"Yes. I saw it on the news this morning. Mr. Durkee, I presume you will expand a bit on that in my Monday morning intelligence briefing?" The President referred to the CIA Director.

"Yes sir, we can give you the down and dirty on the activity in Iran and the status of our rescue mission at any time."

"I assume this is the same squadron of aircraft that our enterprising young captain is from?" The President looked at the Chairman.

"Yes sir, Mr. President. We briefed you on their deployment about six weeks ago. They are an F-4 Phantom squadron out of one of our bases in Germany." The AF CSAF broke in. "They have been flying side by side with the Iranian Air Force, training them in tactics they can use against Saddam Hussein and Iraq. When things blew up in Tehran this morning, the squadron and Air Forces Europe decided to expedite their departure. They bent a few rules but got 23 of the 24 jets out. Nineteen of them made it back to their base in Germany, but four of them had to land at Incirlik, in Turkey, because they missed their refueling time. They can two hop it home tomorrow through Aviano, Italy."

"Why did they miss their tanker? Was it a pilot screw up?" Chief of Staff Taggart piped up. He was about as anti-military as a politician in Washington could be. His question brought a frown to the faces of the military men in the room. The CSAF responded.

"They had to wait until three of the jets were repaired. the flight lead didn't want to leave anyone behind if he didn't have to."

"I get that, but according to CNN that flight leader caused quite a stir when he broke every rule in the book and took off without clearance." Taggart shot back. "Now I understand the whole base is locked down and there are guards on our airplane and people. I hope you are planning on canning the guy?" He drilled his eyes directly into the CSAF, General Furman. Furman just about came out of his skin and was about to jump up and say something he would later regret when the Chairman barged in.

"Mr. Taggart, I assume you've heard the motto 'never leave anyone behind?' It's more of a Marine saying, but it applies to all of our services as well. It's also why we pressed so hard to rescue the missionary. This young captain knew he was faced with giving up four of America's finest fighting machines and the eight crew members who man them. What he did to get out of Iran took a lot of imagination and no shortage of guts. No - we don't plan on disciplining him at all."

"Seems to me the captain ought to be given an air medal and maybe a promotion." This was Director Durkee. He and the President's Chief of Staff had butted heads again.

"Ok. OK gentlemen. Let's stick to the problem at hand." The President chimed in and waved to his Chief of Staff to calm down. "What do you propose now? Have we talked to the ambassador over there yet? And oh by the way, where are we with the Shah's request to come here for his cancer treatments?"

"Mr. President, I have been trying all day to talk to our embassy. The lines of communication out of Tehran have been either severed or at least strictly controlled. I cannot get through to our embassy." SECSTATE Conlin responded. "We did hear from them early on that they were going into a lock down at the embassy and trying to get all Americans loose in the country to come inside the walls. The word on the street and from some of our allies is that it is the Shah's request that has the country up in arms against us. They want him back in Iran for trial and to execute him. We probably should not jump up right away with an invitation to the Shah."

"Ok. I'll think about that. I told him I wanted to help him. How is the roundup of folks to bring into the embassy going?"

"Like I said sir, we have no comm with them now."

"Sir, about the only comm we have into the country is via phone through the USAFE command post to a small command structure inside the IAF F-4 squadron operations building." This was the NSA Chief Mike Nash. "That's how we got the word that the aircraft were airborne early and headed out of country. It was a call set up by the same Iranian pilot, the friend of Captain Mitchell, the flight lead of our four jets parked in Turkey."

"Oh great! So we're relying on some Iranian pilot to tell us what's going on?" Taggart jumped in again. "Seems to me that's cooperating with the enemy. Isn't that tantamount to treason or espionage?"

Everyone in the room just sat there, stunned. The military men shook their heads in disgust. The President just sat there staring ahead waiting for someone else to speak. NSA Director Nash took the lead. "Bobby, you are a horse's ass. The Iranian captain was trying to help. He did help, and in fact he may be our only link of communication with those 14 folks. He also was the source of information that allowed us to rescue Mr. Robertson" He then turned to the President. "Mr. President, I think we need to narrow down the list of people working on this. Our options for recovering those men and that jet are very limited. If I may sir, I suggest we adjourn and The Chairman and I have a proposal that might work."

Carver looked puzzled, but he looked around the room and other than his Chief of Staff, everyone seemed ready to move on. "Ok. My office in 15 minutes." he said and left the room, Taggart tagging along like a puppy dog.

The CSAF took a quick call from his folks in the Air Staff, and before they all left the room he cornered the Chairman and the Assistant SECDEF. "That F-4 on the ramp in Shiraz needs a new engine. We have not been able to squeeze one out of the IAF, even by offering big bucks. Betting on our approval, the USAFE CINC has pulled an engine out of inventory on the base in Aviano. There is also a national guard C-130 on the ramp there and he is having it loaded as we speak to fly it to Incirlik. That way, if we do mount an operation, it will be there ready to go." Ms. Dunlap agreed. "Send it in. If we don't use it, nothing harmed." The three of them, Assistant SECDEF, Chairman of the JCS, CSAF, as well as NSA Chief Nash and CIA's Durkee headed toward the President's office.

Ten minutes later the President and Taggart came into the Oval Office. The staff stood up. "Ok, find a seat folks. What's up?"

Director Durkee spoke first. "Sir I believe you are up to speed on the Tango Team?"

The President looked puzzled then said "I think my predecessor told me a little about it. Some highly sensitive black ops activity, isn't it."

"Yes sir, and we think we need to activate Tango at this time. We can explain, but we need to clear the room of any folks without the need to know." Durkee said, looking at Taggart as he finished the sentence.

Carver looked even more puzzled, then looked around the room. "Who doesn't have the need?"

Everyone looked at Taggart and he became unglued. "That's bull shit! Gentlemen, there isn't anything that the President gets that doesn't come through me first. Now I don't know what this Tango is, but believe me, if the President knows about it, I should too." He stopped and then everyone turned and looked at the President.

Carver paused for a bit, looking deep into the eyes of his top security advisors. Finally he looked at Taggart and said

"Bobby, go ahead and excuse us for a few minutes. If it's anything I think you should be in on, I'll bring you up to speed." *Ah,* the group probably all thought in synch. *The man really does have balls.*

"Mr. President I must protest …" Taggart tried.

"Bobby, I hear you. Now go ahead and step out. I'll talk to you later." The President was even sounding like he had balls. Taggart got up and left in a huff, slamming the door behind him.

Durkee went first. "Mr. President, Tango is a team of highly qualified special operators from all walks of our government. They were first formed during the Cuban missile crisis, then once again when the North Koreans took the USS Pueblo. The attempt then was to rescue the crew. That's sort of the issue here. Tango consists of Army Delta Force personnel, FBI special agents, CIA operatives, Navy UDT operators, and other folks with special skills. They will work directly under your authority, though you may want to appoint one of us or someone else to actually run the operation and keep you in the loop, approving all aspects of the mission."

NSA Director Nash stepped in, "Sir, we believe we need to run a highly clandestine operation to rescue the 14 airmen and hopefully that aircraft, and Tango should handle it. The fewer folks involved the better. There can be no leaks, no compromise of the operation, or we're liable to lose a bunch of good folks. Tango should be given carte blanche for anything and everything they want. That's why they should work for you and within this building."

"Don't y'all think we should try a little diplomacy first?" Carver was getting nervous. These kinds of operations are what got his predecessor's predecessor fired. A little thing called Watergate.

"We have no one to talk to sir. The entire Iranian government is under lock and key. Their leader is in a mansion in the south of France and is persona non grata in his own country. The Ayatollah who appears to be in charge refuses to talk to any international leader right now, and we have no contact with our own ambassador. Diplomacy isn't an option. That's why we didn't invite the Secretary of State here today." Nash spelled it all out.

"Ok, what's your general plan?" The President wanted to know.

The Chairman of the JCS stood up and passed around a few maps and documents stamped "Top Secret" to the President. "The operation will be bit complicated and dependent on a lot of issues, most of all good luck. We should form a Tango Team here this evening. I recommend we use the Vice President's conference room, especially while he is out of the office. Most of the team will depart immediately or in the morning for Incirlik, Turkey. There is a C-130 at Aviano Air Base in Italy being loaded right now with an engine for the crippled F-4 in Shiraz. It will fly directly to Incirlik and meet up with Tango, two large helicopters that the Army is using right now in eastern Turkey to train the Kurds, and the pilot flight leader of the four aircraft from Hahn that diverted to Incirlik earlier. From there the force will quietly deploy to Dhahran, Saudi Arabia, which is the closest friendly air base to Shiraz. They will work out of there for an insertion to deliver the engine, fix the jet, free the hostages, and evacuate the premises. USAFE will also deploy F-16 attack fighters and F-15 air defense birds to Dhahran to support the action. We haven't done much fine tuning. We thought we'd let Tango and USAFE take it from here."

"What kind of timing are you talking about?" The President asked.

"We're thinking we can get everyone to Incirlik by tomorrow and Dhahran by Tuesday. A simulated complex mimicking the tent city and airfield on Shiraz is being constructed now in the desert near Dhahran. The team will practice there Tuesday night and go into Shiraz Wednesday. It will take a few hours to change out the engine on the F-4, but we'll give them a full day. Hopefully then everyone gets on the C-130 Thursday after the jet is fixed. If there are problems with that, the rescue operation would be Thursday night." The Chairman spelled it out.

The President thought a minute, perusing the maps of the area and the list of forces that was proposed. Then he asked "What do you need the pilot of the other airplane for? To fly the repaired one out?"

"Yes sir, and it just so happens the jet will need a Functional Check Flight (FCF), mandatory after an engine change, and Captain Mitchell is FCF qualified." The CSAF answered.

"OK. I guess I should approve this. I really wish there was another way. Couldn't we just get those guys on a commercial flight out of there and 'donate' the F-4 to the Iranians?" The President was waffling.

"In fact they all had tickets to fly out this evening sir, but the tickets were confiscated and the men and one woman are basically under house arrest in their tent city." CSAF said.

"Ok gentlemen. I give up. Go ahead. Chuck, I'd like you to run the show from here. Use whomever you want as military advisor." The President got up to leave. "Let me know when your Tango Team is assembled. I'd like to meet them.

CHAPTER EIGHTEEN

THE WHITE HOUSE - 7 PM

The Tango team arrived at the White House and were ushered into the VP's conference room by the Secret Service. There were two ex-navy UDTs, one currently working at the FBI, the other at the CIA. Two previous Delta Force army guys, and one still on active duty in the Pentagon joined them. In addition, a computer guru and a communications expert, both from the NSA, and a bomb specialist from the FBI rounded out the team present in Washington. Six others were identified and notified at their current locations and were connected into the meeting via phone. They were the pilots and co-pilots of the helicopters presently working with the Kurds in Turkey, and two snipers out of the 82cnd Airborne at Ft. Bragg, North Carolina. The President came in shortly after they all arrived and met everyone. They were briefed not to use their real names and to only use a nickname that they might have or that they could make up. Carver seemed a little put off by that, but he accepted it. He didn't stay around long, simply saying "Good luck and let us know if you need anything."

Richard Durkee took over from there and named Master Sergeant Nolan Ryan, the active duty Army Ranger from the Pentagon, as the team chief. Ryan's "handle" was easy. His namesake being one of the greatest fastball pitchers in major league history, he went by the handle of "Speedball." The rest went through minimum introductions and simply used their nicknames. No one needed to know who they were in real life, just what to call them in this life.

It was quickly established that Speedball, two of the UDTs, and the two Delta Force folks would deploy immediately to Incirlik. There was a CIA executive jet waiting for them at National Airport for a 10 PM takeoff. The two snipers from Ft. Bragg made it to the jet just in time. The communications expert was nicknamed "Quack." Her real name was Maria Duckworth. She issued everyone with the state of the art comm gear - radios that could be used securely and as a phone. They were straight out of the latest James Bond movie, but they were big and heavy - probably why most users called them "bricks." Quack and the computer whiz, "Jailbird," were to fly out the next morning on an Air Force jet to Ramstein Air Base, Germany, home to USAFE Headquarters. They would "chop" (come under the auspices of) to General Walter Bong, the Commander in Chief of USAFE who was the designated commander of the operation.

"Jailbird" came by his name honestly - or maybe it was dishonestly. He's known as one of the best computer hackers in the world. In 1978 computers were in their infancy, so it was easy to hack into them. Johnny Toohey (Jailbird) had done so many times and was creating havoc at the FBI. So they caught him and put him to work, with the "promise" of a lengthy jail sentence if he screwed up. With the team deployed, that left Durkee and one of his own CIA special ops folks in the White House. They were the nucleus of coordination between the guys and gals in the field and the support team at home.

Bobby Taggart couldn't stand the suspense. He had begged the President to let him in on what was going on. Carver told him not to worry, it was nothing to be upset about. Taggart wouldn't keep his nose out of it though, and he managed to sidle up close to Quack as she was leaving the meeting. He introduced himself as the President's "right hand man," told her he was read in on everything and asked her if there was anything she needed. What she needed was a bathroom. He pointed out the nearest ladies room but informed her that it was White House policy that personnel could not take classified information into the restrooms. He told her it was to ensure nothing was destroyed whether inadvertently or on purpose. She said she understood and accepted his offer to keep her briefcase for her while she visited the loo. Quack was hesitant at first, but after all, he was the Chief of Staff - certainly he was read in on everything.

Quack took copious notes - too many for a spook, and unfortunately Taggart was able to get a quick read of the whole plan while she was visiting nature. He had it all neat and tidy when Quack returned, handed it back to her and then left her to go back to his office. He immediately got on the horn to the CIA, then the FBI, and the Pentagon. He used his muscle as the President's man to weasel out enough information to make him dangerous. He learned that a CIA jet was leaving National Airport tonight for Turkey with some special ops folks aboard and a couple of sniper specialists from Ft. Bragg. He also learned that the helicopter mission in northeast Turkey was suspended because the crews were ordered back to Incirlik. Finally, the Pentagon communications center told him of pending deployments from Germany of F-15s and F-16s to Dhahran, Saudi Arabia. Taggart's imagination went wild and he decided to call it a day and head for his favorite watering hole, the bar at the Mayflower Hotel.

INCIRLIK AIR BASE, TURKEY

I was awake early. We managed to get some chow and down a few drinks at the Officer's Club last night. I'd had a call almost immediately after walking into Base Operations after putting our jets to bed. It was from our wing commander at Hahn. He wanted to know "what the fuck did I do to piss off the Iranians when I left Shiraz?" I explained myself as best I could, but I don't think he was very happy. Fortunately Colonel Harwood, his vice commander, was there and witnessed the urgency to get out of Dodge, but the wing king wasn't impressed.

"You get your ass back here tomorrow with those four jets, and don't break any rules doing it." I was ordered.

So our plan was to take off about 0800 and hop into Aviano, Italy, refuel and then go on into Hahn (weather permitting - at least we should be able to get to within Blue Goose range). We were just getting ready to step to the jets when Lt. Col. Watson called for me again. "Grizzly - change of plans." He said. "I can't tell you much but you guys hang tight there in Incirlik. There's a team of spooks coming in there in an exec jet. You need to contact them and basically do what they tell you. This is coming straight from CINC USAFE. Confirm for me though - you basically have three wingmen there right? No flight leads other than yourself?"

"That's basically correct sir, though technically not. Boomer Huston is now a flight lead. I flew his check ride yesterday. Obviously short on flight lead experience, but you know him as well as I do sir, he should be up to whatever we need." I replied.

"Ok. How about your jets? Are they all operational?"

"Yes sir. They're good to go." My curiosity was getting the best of me. "What's going on sir?"

"Not mine to tell you." He answered. "Contact those guys from the private jet. They should be there by now. I'll be seeing you tomorrow."

Now I was really curious. *How is he going to be seeing me tomorrow if he just told us to sit tight?*

I called the Incirlik command post and got the info on the passengers off the executive jet. Their leader was there talking to the Incirlik senior staff and he wanted me to meet him there right away. I told Rhino and the rest of my guys to hang out either at the club or at billeting. I might need to round them up quickly.

I got to the command post post haste and met a grizzled guy with a beard, built like a fireplug, by the name of "Speedball." I also met the Incirlik commander, a one star general who was all serious. I guessed that "Speedball" was the real thing. He had a bunch of folks with him that were just as "interesting" looking and all had nicknames. There was "Grubman" and "Stinker" who were

Army - I guessed Green Berets or Delta Force; There was "Squid" and "Shark" and since "squid" was a handle the UDTs went by, I figured they were both UDTs. Then there was "Longshot" and a woman named "Deadeye." They were the mysterious, not talkative types. I could guess though that with those monickers and the fancy looking rifle cases they were carrying that I probably didn't even want to know what they did for a living. They wanted to know what my "handle" was. I hadn't gathered in my monicker of "Conan" at this time. That came later when I was a squadron commander of an F-16 squadron in Korea. I had been dubbed "Grizzly" during my tour in Southeast Asia, so I tried that out. The gang all snickered and decided "Grizzly" it was.

With the general in the room I was briefed on the coming mission. Our jets were in the process of being reconfigured. They were taking down the centerline fuel tank and adding electronic counter-measure pods, and we were being armed up with Cluster Bomb Munitions (CBU), hot guns with armor piercing rounds, and two AIM-9 heat seeking missiles. This afternoon we were to fly over Syria and Iraq and land at Dhahran Air Base in Saudi Arabia. Diplomatic clearances were being worked to get us through the air space. Four more Sabers from Hahn would meet us there tomorrow, along with 8 F-15s from Bitburg, Germany. "Speedball" and his gang, as well as two helicopters currently in country would meet us in Dhahran as well. In addition, a replacement engine for our crippled bird in Shiraz would be arriving here in Incirlik and then on to Dhahran aboard a National Guard C-130.

The plan was to practice a raid on our Tent City in Shiraz at a site being constructed in the Desert near Dhahran on Tuesday night. Washington was working the diplomatic angle to get us permission to fly me and the spare engine on the C-130 into Shiraz Wednesday morning, give the guys a day to swap it out, and then on Thursday I was supposed to "pretend" to fly a functional test flight, but to actually high tail it south out of Iran to Dhahran. Speedball and his heroes would be on the C-130 as well. They were there as "insurance," though I'm not sure what they would do. Hopefully they'd get everyone aboard to get out of town just as soon as I took off. In the meantime, the helicopters were to sneak into Iran to a spot just south of Shiraz with the same UDT team that rescued Will Robertson. They had just arrived in Bahrain on the USS Virginia and were being transferred into Dhahran via a CIA jet. The F-4s would be ready as a close air support force, and the F-15s would provide top cover for the whole shebang. That's why our jets, and I assumed the ones coming down from Hahn, would be armed with CBU. Cluster Bomb Units are bomb pods that spring open after deployment and spew dozens of high explosive bomblets all around. They are especially devastating for troops in the open, but they'll do a number on vehicles as well. One of the permanent party F-4 pilots at Incirlik, a Major and weapons school graduate, would travel with the spooks to Dhahran to take my cockpit and fly with Rhino on the close air support mission while I was supposedly "stealing back" our wounded bird.

I was impressed with the plan, but I was a bit skeptical that the Iranians now in charge would even let our C-130 in, much less let me fly a test mission on the F-4. With General Ranjahni in custody I didn't think there was anyone at Shiraz who would authorize such a thing. As it turned out, I was right. The diplomatic efforts to get us permission to even be there were unsuccessful. In fact, all they did was alert the HMFsWiC (Head Mother Fuckers What's in Charge) in Tehran to keep a close watch on the yankees down in Shiraz. Fortunately they had no clue what we were up to. The French ambassador to Iran had pleaded to the Ayatollah to allow the U.S. to get their people out. There seemed to be only one hope left - Jani Ranjahni. General Bong at USAFE knew that Jani had helped with the hostage rescue and he also knew that Jani was the son of the Shiraz commander and perhaps had a little pull. I was tasked to get a call in to Jani.

CHAPTER TWENTY

WASHINGTON - MAYFLOWER HOTEL

Bobby Taggart settled into his favorite barstool at the Mayflower cocktail lounge and nestled up to a double bourbon - straight. In fact, he was on his third one and he had passed through the sorrow phase (sorry for himself at not being on the "A" Team this time), and he was now in the pissed off phase. He saw Marianne when she walked in and smiled at her, sucking up his gut, trying to not look so slovenly.

Marianne Rodgers was the new "hot stuff" reporter at the Washington Post. She had only been with the Post about a year, but she knew her way around, and rumor had it that included a few VIP bedrooms. Her most recent triumph had come when she broke the story about a Colorado senator who had been involved with one of his female aides who had turned up dead in a high rent hotel room. Marianne seemed to have an awful lot of personal information on the senator that was of the intimate variety. It didn't hurt that Marianne was a hammer - young, blonde, great body, and legs that wouldn't quit. She recognized Bobby Taggart right away and decided from his apparent mood there might be a story looming. She sat down beside Taggart.

"You look like you're ready to kill somebody." Marianne cooed in Bobby's ear. "What's the matter, is the staff not paying enough attention to their Chief?"

"Marianne Rodgers, right?" Bobby countered. "I saw you come in. You command quite an entrance. Buy you a drink?"

"Sure." She winked at the bartender. "My usual please Ricky." Her usual turned out to whiskey sour, without much whiskey, Bobby noted. "Now seriously Bobby - may I call you Bobby? What's got you ready to spit fire?"

"Oh nothing. Just a matter of some folks forgetting that I have Carver's ear and they have to go through me to bend it." Taggart explained.

"What? Are they making big plans without you? Are we talking domestic issues or foreign?" Her first cast of the fishing line.

"Foreign - something to do with the mess in Iran. "Bobby answered, but quickly decided he might not want to go there. "It's no problem though. Sounds like we have everything in line. I'm sure I'll get the whole story when it gets to be important enough for the President's input."

Marianne smelled a story, but she decided to change the subject and get a little closer to Bobby. What are his interests? Favorite restaurants? Hobbies? Small talk to get him comfortable. She knew Taggart was divorced and she also knew that she could pretty much have him whenever she wanted. After about 11:30 they'd pretty much covered everything she knew to lead with and she watched Taggart put down a few more double Jacks. She figured she needed to make her move before he fell asleep on her. She put her hand on Bobby's inner thigh and moved it up a little close to "Mr. Johnson."

"Bobby, I keep a room here at the Mayflower and I'm getting really horny right now. How about you?"

"Uh, yeah. I think that would be pretty nice." Bobby said and leaned in to get a kiss. Marianne gave him a peck on the lips and stood up.

"Ricky - would you put all this on my tab?" She said to the bartender.

"Er no. Actually, I can't let you do that. Let me treat." Bobby jumped in, still sober enough to know he couldn't owe her anything witnessed in public.

"Oh. I forgot. No problem. I wouldn't want to get the President's Chief of Staff in trouble." She said too loud to Bobby's liking. "Let's just split it up." They each paid for their drinks and Bobby left a big tip while looking at Ricky and putting his finger to his lips with a "Sssh." They left the bar and caught the first elevator up.

When they got to Marianne's room Bobby went to work. He pressed up against her while kissing her neck and trying to unzip her dress. Marianne played along for a bit, enough to get him really aroused, then gently pushed him away and said "Slow down Tiger. Tell you what. There's a mini-bar there in the credenza. Fix yourself another drink while I take care of some girly stuff." She headed toward the bathroom and said "I'll be right back." Bobby poured himself a hefty whiskey and downed it quickly, thinking

Marianne would be walking in soon in the all together. Marianne in the meantime, waited long enough for Taggart to refill his glass and let her hair down. She slipped into a cute little ditty that she kept hanging in the bathroom for just these kinds of situations. She came out with a "Ta Dah!" and Bobby was blown away.

Marianne guided the activity to her speed. Bobby was ready to jump right on and do the deed, but she wanted to go slow and easy and work her magic on the klutz so he'd be eating out of her palm in no time. She let him screw her and reacted with an academy award performance, giving Bobby the idea he was the best she'd ever had. In fact, she hated this part of her job and just wanted to get it over with, so as he rolled off gasping for breath she cast in another fishing line. "So Bobby, tell me. What are we going to do about Iran? Isn't the whole thing their own problem? Why should we care?"

Bobby was not in any shape to think about what he was saying or doing. He just blurted out "Well, it seems we have a couple dozen Air Force types down in the southern part of their country and we need to get them out. The Iranian army over there is basically holding them hostage. But not to worry, we're assembling a team of special ops to go in and rescue them."

"Wow! When does all this happen? And Bobby, tell me about the rescue of the missionary kid." She pushed. Bobby all of a sudden sobered up and realized he'd said too much. *Goddamn the President for not keeping me in the loop!*

"Look Marianne, I shouldn't have told you all of this. I think we'd better change the subject." Bobby pleaded.

"No problem Tiger. You didn't tell me enough fo run with anyway." She let him off the hook, sort of. "But tell you what. How about giving me the first whack when there is a story? Don't you think I deserve that?" She rolled over and gave him a nice long kiss.

"Yeah sure. I can do that. I'll call you as soon as I can. Now, how about another round?" She had aroused Mr. Johnson again.

"Oh Bobby. You're an animal. I really don't think I can. You did me in. Besides, it's getting late and a girl's got to get her beauty sleep you know." She rolled out of bed and playfully tossed his underwear at him as she went back to the bathroom. Bobby took the hint, got up and got dressed, and snuck in one more nice kiss before she shooed him out the door.

CHAPTER TWENTY ONE
INCIRLIK AIR BASE

After a lot of machinations and frustrations I was able to get in contact with Jani on a commercial line to his squadron building. He told me things are really tense around the base. His squadron has been told to either go home to their families or sit in the building, but not to try to fly or anything else. Their families and the whole local populace were told to stay in their homes - not to go shopping for anything outside. Although there wasn't a martial law declared, it felt that way. Jani had stayed at the squadron building to try and see his father. His squadron commander had a little pull with the army general in charge of the "lock down," but so far he wouldn't budge on access to General Ranjahni. The general was being kept in his office - not exactly a "prisoner," but unable to contact anyone or leave his office. There were two guards in the office with him.

"That sure sounds like he's a prisoner to me." I said to Jani.

"Me also, but there doesn't seem to be anyone who will listen. Did you get into any trouble when you left here with your 'communications problems'?" Jani asked.

"A little, but now I've got a bigger problem. We need to get our people out of there." I said.

I explained the situation to Jani, leaving out a whole lot, like the fact we were getting ready to raid Shiraz and rescue the hostages. I basically said we would like to trade a perfectly operational F-4 (the one on his ramp) for our 14 airmen. We would bring in a C-130 tomorrow with a replacement engine, our crew would make the swap out, and I would be there to do a functional check flight (FCF) before turning it over to them. Then the 14 airmen and I would get on the C-130 and be gone within 24 hours. Fortunately he understood about the aircraft needing an FCF after an engine change. They did the same thing in their Air Force.

"I'm not sure they would let you fly it. You've already made a name for yourself around here. Why couldn't one of our FCF pilots check it out?" Jani offered. He didn't seem real optimistic about the whole plan.

I thought a minute, then lied, "Well, if it doesn't pass the test we wouldn't want to endanger one of your pilots, anymore than we want to hand over a crippled jet to you. I will fly it solo like we do with our own FCFs, so there shouldn't be a concern about me sneaking out of town without a back seater and navigator." In fact, we do fly our FCF missions without a back seater. I basically turn on the radar and the inertial navigation system (INS) before I get in and crank up. We strap down the seat and don't worry about the lack of accuracy we get without sufficient warm up time on the INS. We only fly FCF missions on clear and sunny days and don't have to navigate much. As I thought about all that it struck me I would have a fine time sneaking south and out of the country without a real navigation system. I would miss Rhino not being there, but I also felt confident that I could do it in the daylight. Hopefully it would still be daytime.

Like I said, Jani was not optimistic. In fact, he didn't want to rock the boat anymore than he already had about seeing his father. He didn't even know who they would talk to that would have the authority to make a deal. I impressed upon him the value of the jet - millions of dollars, and one less the IAF would have to buy from us. I also hinted that unless things got much better real soon, they probably wouldn't be able to buy anymore goodies from the U.S.

"Let me talk to my squadron commander." Jani offered. "He might have a different outlook on this whole thing, and he might at least know who to talk to. I'll call you back within an hour."

I hung up with Jani and conferred with Speedball and the Incirlik brass. I had a thought.

"Do you think there's a way we could sweeten the deal?" I asked, not knowing exactly who to ask. Speedball seemed to be running the show.

"What do you mean, offer them another airplane or two?" Speedball asked back.

"How about money? What if we offered them basically a ransom of the jet and a few million dollars." I was way out of my element here. I knew that it has always been the policy of the U.S. not to negotiate with terrorists, but at this point at least, the new government in Iran weren't exactly terrorists.

There was a pregnant pause, then General Tom Blackburn, the Incirlik wing commander finally spoke. He had been sort of in the background during all of this. "I think we'd better run that one up the flagpole to General Bong at USAFE HQ. Are you thinking we'll need to offer more than just the jet?"

"I don't know sir, but my guy over there in Shiraz doesn't seem very optimistic and it seems the biggest problem they have is who to talk to. But the way I see it, money talks. We could wave a big number at them and maybe the army big cheese in charge of the situation there would see a way to enhance his career —- or maybe his own pocket. It could be just a ploy anyway. We could promise to deliver a bunch of coin as soon as our guys are outbound and just not do it. I could set up some kind of ruse where they could find the money after we are on the C-130 outbound, and make it a bag full of monopoly money for that matter." I was on a roll now, setting up a James Bond scenario, or maybe Tom Clancy. Anyway, they didn't completely poo-poo the idea and General Blackburn called USAFE.

In the meantime, the four other players in the game came in. The HH-53 choppers and their two pilots each. They introduced themselves as "Wop," a diminutive woman with obvious Italian lineage, the pilot of one chopper and her co-pilot "Gronk" - big guy. They looked like Chewy and Leia from Star Wars. The other bird was flown by "Red Baron" and "Snoopy." I love these call signs. They were quickly briefed and sent on their way to make it down to Dhahran. Since diplomacy was a bit sticky, especially with Syria, it was decided they would take two nights to get there, and take a circuitous route to get through Syria and Iraq. The main problem was that the Syrians were not real happy with the U.S. support of the Kurds, and it was not difficult to figure that these two helicopters had been part of Kurd aid campaign.

CINC USAFE was "sort of" impressed with our plan, but he had to run the whole thing up the flagpole in Washington. I was concerned it was all going to take too long, and sure enough, Jani called me back. He had his squadron commander, Lt. Colonel Hassan, on the line with him.

"So Captain Mitchell, Jani tells me you have a plan to try and get your people out of here." He said. "I must admit, it is very tempting to have another F-4 in our inventory, but I'm not sure I can convince the people in charge of our country right now."

"I understand sir. We have no way of contacting your new government and really no way of discussing anything with anyone. Sir, how well do you know the army general who is running things there? Can you talk to him?" I queried.

"Ha! General Rashid is a puppet, as are most of the military leaders behind this coup. They all are riding this wave of new radicalism and simply doing what they are told. I know Rashid from our days at the military academy. I don't trust him, but I also know some things about him he wishes I didn't." That peaked my interest.

I went out on a limb I had no business climbing. "What if in addition to the F-4 my government offered cash for the release of our people? I could bring it with me and give it to General Rashid. We could do it without any announcement to Tehran and he could do whatever he wants with the money."

"How much money are you talking about?" Hassan asked.

I was in way over my head now, so *What the hell!* "How about 14 million dollars - a million for each man being held?"

Hassan thought about it for a while, then said. "It is an interesting concept Captain Mitchell, but tell me, are you in a position to make such an offer?"

"I believe so sir. I have discussed with our Commander in Chief and he is on board." It was a complete lie. I had discussed with our USAFE Commander in Chief - just not the final Commander in Chief, President Carver. And Bong wasn't necessarily "on board," he just hadn't said no.

"All right, I will present the offer to General Rashid. In the meantime, I think you can probably continue to plan to bring in an engine to fix the jet on our ramp. It is simply taking up space out there now." Hassan came back. "When are you planning on coming?"

"We would be there with a C-130 and engine on Wednesday sir. Our people could probably have it repaired in a few hours, but I would suggest we give them 24 hours and I would test fly the airplane on Thursday. We could leave that evening." About now I was wondering how much deep shit I had gotten myself into.

"Alright, fine. We will call you back tomorrow to confirm whatever it is we're going to do." Hassan then hung up.

I hung up and briefed General Blackburn and Speedball and hustled off to meet my guys at Base Operations. Rhino had filed our flight plan to Dahran and made a couple of phone calls to assure we could cross Syria and Iraq. Since we weren't really in any kind of conflict with either of them, we got clearance. They took us on a bit of an indirect routing and we would arrive at Dahran with minimum fuel, but the weather was supposed to be good on our arrival, so we went. I let Bosco lead this mission as one of his flight lead checkout rides. He did well, and is one step closer to becoming another experienced Saber flight lead.

CHAPTER TWENTY TWO
WASHINGTON

The front page headline of the Washington Post was full of a lot of speculation or false reporting, but enough truth to do major damage to the plan to get our folks out of Shiraz. Marianne Rodgers had her name on the byline and Bobby Taggart had indigestion. The rest of the senior staff in the administration were furious, trying decide who among them sprung the leak.

"**U.S. To Mount Mission to Rescue USAF Hostages in Iran.**" Ouch! That hurts. The story went on to say that we had 14 airmen stuck on the ground at Shiraz and we were about to launch a rescue mission that was being organized and led by a highly clandestine team of special operations folks working directly from the White House. There were no specifics of the plan (simply because Marianne didn't know anything about the plan). However, the fact that this super secret black ops group existed and that they were planning what could be construed as an act of war without Congress knowing a thing about it, rankled the politicians - especially in the opposition Republican Party. The Secretary of Defense especially was livid and he called Bobby

Taggart to set up an emergency meeting of the President's inner circle in the know about Tango. Taggart was pissed as well, but obviously for different reasons and he really didn't want to get that group together with the President, especially if they were going to try and ferret out where the leak to Marianne Rodgers came from. He knew however, that to deny the meeting would simply raise the suspicions of the SECDEF and others.

The meeting took place at 10 AM in the White House Situation Room. Taggart had to cancel a meeting Carver was to have with the Congressional Black Caucus, but he figured that wouldn't be much fun for the President anyway. Everyone was there that were read in on the Tango Team and the pending rescue attempt - Director Durkee, Chairman Admiral Miller, NSA Chief Nash, CSAF General Furman. Secretary of Defense Lawrence Malloy had returned from his trip and was there as well. Durkee had called SECSTATE Conlin and suggested he attend as well. Although he wasn't in on forming up the Tango Team, it was likely there were going to be some diplomatic fences to mend. Chief of White House Staff Taggart was there as well, hoping he could sit in on this meeting.

"Y'all be seated please." The President said when he entered the room. He looked around to see who was there and seemed satisfied. "So where do we suppose the leak to Marianne Rodgers came from?" The million dollar question.

"Mr. President, I don't think any of us knows the answer to that." Durkee jumped right in. "Since the story is lacking in facts and specifics, I personally think it was someone who is on the periphery - one of our aides or staff." Taggart squirmed in his chair and he could swear Durkee was aiming at him. "Which reminds me sir." Durkee continued. "If we are going to discuss the matter any further we probably should clear the room of folks not read in on the operation. However, I took the liberty to invite Secretary Conlin. I think there will need to be some level of diplomacy needed now to try and defuse the mission."

The President nodded and said "God point Dick," and looking at Taggart said "Bobby would you excuse us please?"

Jumping up to appear innocent, Bobby said "Of course sir, I'll be right outside if you need anything."

"So tell me Richard, how bad is it? Will we have to scrub the mission?" Carver asked Durkee.

"I think not Mr. President." It was National Security Advisor Mike Nash. "Although the heads of the mob in Tehran now know that we have folks in the country, and that we might be trying to get them out, they don't have many specifics or ideas of the timing. At least we hope not. That's the problem, we don't have anyone over there we can talk too."

Carver looked at his Secretary of State. "Tim, what do you think, or I guess more importantly, what does your ambassador think?"

"I just talked to him this morning sir. It's Ambassador Joseph Schultz. He is not able to confer with anyone in charge or even anyone who used to be in charge in Tehran." Conlin responded. "Most of them are either in jail or under house arrest with no contact to the outside. Others have simply disappeared. I asked him about the story in the Post, but he had not heard of anything. I don't think he knew we still had people in Shiraz. Since I was not privy to the planning going on, it was all a surprise to me too." The Secretary looked like a sick puppy.

"Sorry about that Tim. We were trying to keep the numbers down about this rescue mission." The President came back. "But I guess it didn't matter. Are we still planning something?" Carver looked at Durkee and Nash.

"We think we still have a chance of getting those folks out sir." Nash replied. "The Tango leader is now in Turkey, leaving later today for Dhahran. The pilot who led our last formation out of country evidently has a contact in the IAF there in Shiraz and has communicated with him. The IAF squadron commander on the base in Shiraz in turn has a bit of a relationship with the army general who has locked the base down. General Bong in Ramstein believes this mission can still work, but we may have to sweeten the pot in our offer to 'buy the freedom' of our people. We have extended your idea of giving the Iranians our sick bird on their ramp, but someone has come up with an idea of offering money as well."

"Sir, I believe that would be a big mistake." It was CIA Director Durkee. "We have long held onto the policy of not negotiating with terrorists."

"I understand Dick, but are these people really terrorists? We didn't even know who they were, and so far I think they are only beating up on their own people." The President responded. "Who's idea was the money side, and how much are we talking about?" He looked back at Nash.

"General Bong brought it up this morning. I don't know who's brainchild it was. Perhaps the Tango Team." Nash replied. "Anyway, the number bantered around is $14 million, one million for each of the airmen stuck there. I will try and contact our Tango Team leader and see what he knows, and if he thinks it will even work."

"OK. I'm not big on ransom money, but if we think it will work, I suppose it's better than just raiding the place and starting a skirmish." The President surmised. "What do we do about this news story and how should we respond to all the questions we are certain to get?"

"Sir, my recommendation is to simply deny there is any clandestine plan in the works, but that we are working through diplomatic channels to gain the release of our people." It was Durkee and he looked at SECSTATE Conlin.

"That's all fine and good Dick, but we really don't have any diplomatic channels to work through. Right now I'm worried about our citizens in Tehran. Including families of our embassy workers, there are literally hundreds of Americans in Tehran. Because of the protests and threats we have experienced at the embassy, I've directed Ambassador Schultz to evacuate all dependents and as much of the staff as he can, and to contact other private business folks to do the same." Conlin offered. "I suppose we can add these 14 airmen to the list of folks we'd like to get on an airliner."

"Ok Tim. I agree. Spend your time on the folks in Tehran and elsewhere. We'll play dumb to any questions about a raid." The President stood up to leave. "Let me know after you've done your practice tomorrow and everything is ready. I think we want to just do a trade for the airplane and let our people get out on that cargo plane bringing in the engine. I'm not inclined to add money to the ante, but if we get an indication that's what is required, let's look at it then." At that he left the room.

SECDEF Durkee, NSA Nash and CIA Director Malloy huddled with Chairman Miller and General Furman. Miller ran down the specifics of the plan as it had unfolded so far. "Gentlemen, I think we have to plan for the worst while hoping for the best." He explained. "If everything goes well and the Iranians think an operational multi-million dollar airplane is a good trade for our folks, great. Even if by adding $14 million to the deal those guys get on that C-130, we will have dodged a bullet. But I think we continue planning for a rescue operation. The F-4s and F-15s from our European bases are en route to Dhahran, The two helicopters and the C-130 with the engine are also on their way. We have the carrier Enterprise in Oman right now on a port of call visit. Her armada is out in the northwest area of the Indian ocean. The entire Iranian Navy is out in the gulf right now. They just finished up a big exercise last week that our F-4 squadron participated in just before they left on Sunday. If things get tense and the water gets too hot, I think we might need to have a presence out there."

General Furman had hooked up General Bong on the phone from Ramstein, and addressed him. "Walter, you've heard all of this. Are you on board?"

"Yes sir and I agree with Admiral Miller. I don't have much faith in a peaceful resolution here. We are basically taking the word of one of our Air Force captains who's in touch with an Iranian captain that the army in Shiraz will cooperate." Bong responded. "This 'Speedball' guy you sent over in charge of the whole shebang is also preparing for the worst. I plan on flying down to Incirlik myself and I'll take the Tango Team's computer and communications people with me. The Incirlk command center isn't as sophisticated as my own here, but at least they are in tune with the region. I basically have nothing but phone comm with them from here."

General Bong was a fighter pilot with thousands of hours in the F-4 and earlier fighters, with tours in Vietnam. His father was Dick Bong, America's number one ace during WWII in the Pacific. General Bong was itching for a fight. He knew he wouldn't be in it, but he was a great leader and organizer.

"Good idea Walter." Furman said and with a nod from Admiral Miller and SECDEF Durkee declared "You've got the wheel on this thing. Brief us in on what you're planning, but I think you can count on the President going along with whatever you decide needs to be done."

"Thank you sr. I'll check in when I get set up in Turkey."

CHAPTER TWENTY THREE

DHAHRAN, SAUDI ARABIA

Everyone was in place. Lt. Colonel Watson had brought down five of our F4s from Hahn, making nine to get eight airborne when it came time for the mission. Major Luke Shivner, the permanent party pilot from Incirlik came down aboard the C-130 and was integrated into the plan. He was set up to fly with Rhino as number three and deputy lead in Watson's flight of four. Tony Gilford was to lead the other four ship. Nine F-15s from the 22cnd Tactical Fighter Squadron in Bitburg arrived as well. Leading one of their flights was my old friend and roommate from southeast Asia, Pete Trask. It was good to see him again, but we would have liked better circumstances. The C-130 had arrived with Shivner and the engine. The crew were Air National Guard guys from the Arkansas Guard. The pilot had experience in Vietnam and his co-pilot was also very experienced, though an American Airlines pilot in real life.

Speedball and his group were all present and the UDT team had been shuttled over from the USS Virginia in Bahrain. Speedball also was in communication with the captains of a destroyer and the Virginia. A unit of the Navy Seabees out of Norfolk were in Saudi Arabia, working with the Saudi army building quick reaction temporary runways in the desert out of PCP mesh steel. Speedball used his late acquired authority and had them moved to Dhahran as well. They were out west of the city with a couple of the Tango Team members erecting a makeshift model of the USAF Tent City in Shiraz. Tonight we were going to practice an extraction mission to free a bunch of "hostages" being guarded by Saudi regular army.

Speedball called everyone together at 1400 hours. Everyone arrived a little early and made introductions. Just the flight leads of the fighter units were present.

"Ok folks, here's what we've planned up so far." Speedball announced. "General Bong is en route to Incirlik and will take command of the operation should it dissolve into a military conflict. We are going to be ready and in fact practice that much of it tonight. Do you fighter jocks want to be in on this practice? We are basically going to raid the Tent City and get the hostages out assuming they aren't allowed a seat on the C-130." Speedball asked Lt. Colonel Watson and the Pete Trask.

"I think we'd be better off just doing some target study on laying down close air support once you're on the ground." Colonel Watson said. "It won't do us much good to blow away a bunch of plywood and cardboard tonight"

"If we are supposed to provide cover for the helicopters I think we'd like to practice that tonight." Trask said. "We're not used to supporting slow movers that much, and we could use the coordination practice."

"Ok. Sounds good. I'll let you discuss it with the chopper pilots when we're done here." Speedball said.

About the time we were getting deep into the mission planning I got a call from Jani and Lt. Colonel Hassan.

"It seems I was right about General Rashid." Hassan said. "He is anxious on getting his greedy hands on the money. In the meantime he says he will pass the info on the trade for the F-4 up to Tehran. He seems to think they will approve. I don't know if that is really the case or if he realizes that the only way he will get his money is if you come in with the intention of fixing the jet as well."

I wasn't sure how to react since the money transaction had not been approved. In fact, I had heard that the President is not looking favorably on it. But I was stuck between a rock and a hard place. I thought *to hell with it. I'm not going to leave them any money anyway, but if I don't tell them I will, we won't get off the ground.*

"Ok. Good sir. I will arrive early afternoon tomorrow on a C-130 with the engine. Our folks there will change it out, and I will plan on flying the check flight Thursday afternoon. Once I land and we are all aboard the C-130, I'll tell you where to find the money." I replied. "Thank you for your help Colonel Hassan. I hope you and Jani will come out of this ok. Jani - how is your family? Are you able to move about the city or base?"

"We will be ok." Terse, to the point. Obviously Jani didn't want to discuss anything further in front of his commander.

I let it drop. "Ok. I'll see you tomorrow."

"Until then." Jani signed off in a hurry.

The plan was fleshed out amongst the players. The guard guys would fly the engine and me into Shiraz about noon on Wednesday. Grubman, Stinker, Squid and Sniper will also be on board dressed as Arkansas Guard airmen. Shaves and haircuts were in store for most of them tonight. They will help unload the engine and basically melt into the crowd of airman at the base. Hahn maintenance folks will change out the engine and then pack all their stuff aboard the C-130.

I will take off on the "Functional (maybe 'Fictional') Check Flight" about 5 PM on Thursday. I will put on a show. A couple of high speed passes over the airfield, a slow speed pass with the landing gear down, and hopefully, while everyone is watching, the crew will all climb aboard the C-130, and then they will take off with minimum communications. I will then radio to Jani Ranjahni at his squadron where to tell General Rashid to find his money - in a trunk inside the main tent in our Tent City. Then I'll zoom to high altitude to preserve my fuel and head south to Dhahran. The choppers will launch at midnight Wednesday night and go in hugging the terrain to a wadi behind a ridge line about 20 miles south of Shiraz. They will have Speedball and Longshot and the Navy UDT team on board, and they will hunker down there in case they're needed. The fighter squadrons will launch from Dhahran about 5 PM and set up to support. The F-4s will orbit just off shore waiting for cries for help to go in and make a mess of Shiraz Air Base. The F-15s will split up. Four of them will hang loose over the gulf until the choppers start out, then they'll "escort" the choppers or at least provide top cover. Two of the other

Eagles will rendezvous with me at altitude and provide escort for my Phantom. The other two will zoom in and provide escort for the C-130. If all goes well we should all be back in the nest on Dhahran Air Base by 8 PM.

If all doesn't go well and the Iranians cause problems, the Tango Team that came in on the C-130 will gather all the airmen in one place and set up a perimeter defense around them. The choppers will blow in as quick as they can. They will put down on the southern edge of Tent City next to the perimeter of the base fence and the UDTs and Longshot will deploy. Speedball will stay aboard and communicate with the others to get them on board the choppers as soon as possible. Once loaded, the choppers will head south while the Sabers will come in and blow down some tents, and buildings, and Iranian army guys with their CBU. The F-15s will hang out looking for any brave but stupid IAF fighter pilot that might try to be a hero. If that's the way it goes, it might take us a little while longer to all congregate at a bar someplace in Dhahran afterward.

The practice went fairly well that night. I had minimum input and little to do. My part would simply be to get out of the way with the phantom. Dust was a big issue - at least in the desert of Saudi Arabia it was. Wop and Red Baron did a little target study to find the best places to land without obliterating everyone's visibility. Out in the the wadi south of the base it was simple. They just separated themselves on landing. Near the Tent City though it could be tough. It was decided that all of the UDTs and Longshot would be in the first chopper and actually land at the other side of the complex. Red Baron's chopper would set down at the near side and set up to take all of the passengers.

The Eagle drivers coordinated with the choppers going in and coming out of the practice run. It was determined that their best bet was to hold at about 5000 feet and offset the helicopters so that they could watch for bad guys while not highlighting where the HH-53s were. They split their four ship flights into two ships at opposite ends of a racetrack orbit. They would adjust the pattern so it moved across the ground about the speed the choppers were flying - a couple miles per minute

CHAPTER TWENTY FOUR
BUSHEHR, IRAN

The Persian Princess was all lit up and it was evident she was being prepared for launch. Food, drink and other supplies were brought aboard. Already on board were the four bodyguards who had accompanied us on our "fishing" trip and the two guards from Will Robertson's jail. In addition, at about 11 PM a truck with a cover on the back drove up and five passengers got out and quietly boarded the Princess. They looked to be three women clad in burkas and cloaks and two children holding their mother's hands. They boarded, and shortly after the Persian Princess cast off for parts unknown.

In the meantime, about a half block away where the fishing boats were moored a similar group of "passengers" boarded one of the trawlers under the cloak of darkness, being careful not to be seen while still making haste to get below and hidden. They were Jani Ranjahni's mother, grandmother, her aunt, and her aunt's two kids. Jani and his father had set it up to get the family out of the country. Unfortunately there wasn't room for more folks, like

Jani's wife and kids, but it became apparent Jani had other plans for them.

Jani's uncle, his mother's sister's husband, was against this whole clandestine operation. In fact, he threatened to pull the plug on it by telling the authorities the plan. Jani's father got involved and was able to arrange an office visit with his wife's brother-in-law. It wasn't exactly a "visit," more like an ass chewing and threats of dire circumstances. Uncle left the meeting scared to death, but understanding that he had one mission that evening - to alert the authorities to the getaway .... of the Persian Princess. That he did the next morning and the army and navy sent out a search and destroy mission after the Princess that was sailing northwest up the Gulf. The intercept took place about noon the day we were to fly the coop. By the time it was obvious that the family was not on board, the small fishing trawler was half way across the Gulf towards Dhahran.

Once within the maritime boundaries of Saudi Arabia the captain of the fishing vessel declared an emergency SOS that he was taking on water. In the meantime, the gang that intercepted the Princess had radioed back that they had been tricked, and the Iranian navy was put on alert to intercept any vessels that had departed Iran. Two forces met at the fishing trawler within minutes of each other - the Saudi Coast Guard and the Iranian Navy. Although the Iranians possessed a lot more firepower, they realized, and it was impressed upon them by the Saudis, that they were inside Saudi jurisdiction. The Iranians backed off and the fishing trawler was towed into port near Dhahran. The family was discovered and immediately arrested under custody of the Saudi government.

CHAPTER TWENTY FIVE

WASHINGTON

Bobby Taggart was really pissed tonight. He wasn't sure if he wanted to run into Marianne Rodgers or not. The horny part of him wouldn't mind another romp in the hay, but the pissed off part of him wanted to rag all over her for betraying his trust - or something like that. He was still pissed at not really knowing anything about the President's plans either. As it turned out, it didn't matter. In she walked, dressed to the nines on the arm of somebody new. Bobby recognized the man. He was Tom Tyler, military aide de camp to the Secretary of Defense. Tom was a major in the Air Force, but today he was dressed in a Gucci suit and new Italian shoes.

They sat in a booth just across the bar from Bobby and he noticed that Marianne recognized he was there. She smiled and then cuddled up to her new toy and purred in his ear. Taggart came unglued.

"Well, well." Taggart said as he came up to the couple while chugging the fourth of his double whiskeys of the night. "What have we here? Hello miss Rodgers, you're looking dazzling tonight.

Isn't she Major? Tell me Marianne, is this the source of your news that was in your story this morning? You'd better be careful Major Tyler, I hear she has a habit of kissing and telling — or is it kissing and writing?"

Tyler turned white as a ghost. He knew who Taggart was. Anyone who had been in the White House knew who Taggart was, but he didn't think anyone would recognize himself out of uniform. He hadn't really thought about the Post article this morning. He just reacted like any red blooded American boy would when Marianne had sidled up to him as he was leaving the Pentagon this evening. He had seen her there before and knew it was part of her "beat," but he hadn't made the connection to the story. He suddenly got real nervous and pulled away from Marianne, leaning back in his seat. He was about to say something stupid when Marianne beat him to it.

"Good evening to you too Bobby. What's the matter? You're not jealous are you? I didn't know you were acquainted with Tom here. Would you like to join us? I always wondered what a triage would be like. Or is that the right word? You know - two on one. I know you could use some help, but I've got the feeling that Tom here can hold his own without any help. Right Tom?" Marianne slid over closer to Tom and grabbed his hand.

"You stupid bitch! You don't have a clue what you're talking about and judging from this morning's story, you know even less about what you write." Bobby was on a roll. "Major, I'd be very careful about any pillow talk y'all might have tonight. You might read about it as a fiction novel in tomorrow's Post." Bobby started to walk away.

"Don't get all jealous and upset Mr. Taggart." Marianne called after him as she got up from the table. In loud enough shouts that everyone in the Mayflower bar could hear, she yelled "You should really be careful about the information you share after you've had a few too many. In your position you might be giving away state secrets."

"Why you…" Bobby had lost it and was heading back to really make things worse when Ricky, the bartender stepped in and grabbed him.

"Whoa Mr. Taggart. Come on. Let me put you in a cab. You don't need this and frankly, neither does the Mayflower."

Bobby stood there with fire in his eyes for a minute or so with Marianne Rodgers matching him stare for stare. In the meantime, Tom Tyler took the opportunity to squeeze out of the booth and head for the door. Marianne saw him and roared out laughing. "I'm really beginning to wonder if there are any real men in this town. Let him go Ricky. He knows better than to push this any further." She sat back down at her table and downed her drink.

Taggart shook loose of the bartender and picked up his coat from the chair he'd thrown it over when he came in. He put it on all the while watching Marianne as she basically ignored him. She looked up as he was leaving and threw him a kiss and a wink. He mouthed the words "I'll get you!" and left.

The next morning the headline of the Washington Post was a lot different. **"Post Reporter Found Dead at the Mayflower."** It seemed that sometime around midnight Marianne Rodgers was found in a heap of blood and broken bones on the pool deck beneath her room in the hotel. It looked like she had done a swan dive off her 12th floor balcony. There was a note found in her room that was typed from a word processor. It explained that she was distraught over a lost lover and at not being promoted in her job.

The D.C. police investigated the scene and her room, and found nothing disturbed, no signs of a struggle and no other marks on her body. On the surface, it looked like a suicide, but since Ms. Rodgers had made a lot of enemies in her time as a reporter, it was turned over to the best homicide detective the city had, Detective Sergeant Duke Welch. The Post story on Thursday didn't go into much detail since the story had just broken. Bobby Taggart kept a low profile around the White House, not ducking but not contributing to any conversations about the incident.

Tom Tyler also avoided any discussions about the topic, and since he was a married man, he decided he would avoid the subject as much as he could.

CHAPTER TWENTY SIX
DHAHRAN

I spent the morning reviewing maps of the territory south of Shiraz and across the Persian Gulf to Dhahran. I was going to have to navigate my way without much of an inertial navigation system and decided to familiarize myself with the route.

At about ten o'clock I had a shocker of a phone call. It was from Jani Ranjahni. "Brad, I have a proposal for you."

"Hey Jani, what's up? I'm just getting ready to go climb aboard the C-130." I responded.

"I want you to take my family and my father out with you when you go. We do not want to live in an Iran with the Ayatollah in power. I want to raise my children in the west, and my father most certainly faces execution if he stays here."

I was flabbergasted. This was a twist that most surely will result in a fight when we try to pull it off. IF we tried to pull it off. I knew that decisions like this were well above my pay grade, but I didn't know who to turn to. "Holy shit Jani! Wow! I can certainly understand your predicament, but I don't have the authority to make it happen. There's no way I could get an approval which would probably have to come from the White House. I'm supposed to take off here in a couple hours."

"Brad, I don't care who you have to talk to or how you plan on doing it, but I will just say you either take us out with you or this whole plan will fall apart." Jani countered.

"What do you mean 'fall apart'?" I asked. "Are you going to spill the beans? Does your squadron commander know about this?"

"No. No one knows. Not even my father, and he may even resist, but we will have to force him to leave and not to be a martyr. Yes - if you don't at least agree to try to get us out, I will alert the authorities about this venture." Jani had me at a huge disadvantage.

"OK. OK. I'll raise the question. But I won't be able to know the answer until later today when I arrive." I said.

"OK, I will see you when you land. Hopefully you will have good news."

My first stop was to see Colonel Watson. He has always been like a role model for me - the type of squadron commander I'd like to be if I ever get that far. I value his opinion, even though this isn't an issue he's probably used to facing. I told him about Jani's edict as well as my dangling the offer of a ransom under the nose of the general in charge of the lockdown at Shiraz.

"Jesus Christ Mitchell, you sure landed in the shit on this one." He said. "I haven't heard anything about a monetary payment to get our guys out. Have you driven it by the higher ups? General Bong? D.C.?"

"Yes sir. We discussed it with General Bong when I was up in Incirlik and he was going to pose it to the Pentagon and I guess the President." I answered, "But I haven't heard anything back. My plan was to simply do what I went out on a limb and did already - tell General Rashid that I would be bringing in $14 million and would tell him where to find it once we're all airborne out of there. I thought about putting a bunch of monopoly money in a bag, but I figure that would piss him off even more than having nothing there."

"So you decided on playing a hoax on him? Holy shit! You're right, you have gone out on a limb and I don't think the limb can come close to holding your weight. Boy, you'd better hope everyone gets out before he discovers the truth. All hell could break loose."

"Yeah, I guess you're right on that, but in my discussions with Jani's squadron commander, who knows this General Rashid, he said that he didn't think the general would go for a swap for just the jet on their ramp." I said. "He believes this general is a greedy bastard and with the offer to grease his palm, we might actually be allowed off the base. I think we're too far down the road to alter that part of this fiasco."

"I suppose you're right. Does this 'Speedball' guy know about this?" Watson countered.

"Yes, but not about Jani's latest demand. I guess I'll go see him next."

"Good idea. You want some top cover?" Watson asked.

"Yes sir. Thanks. I might need you to pick up the pieces."

We caught up with Speedball in a makeshift command post which is just a room in one wing of the Saudi Air Force building next to the flight line. I reiterated my problem and reminded him that I was supposed to be on the C-130 inbound to Shiraz in less than an hour.

"God damn Air Force, you're getting good at throwing wrenches in the gears of this thing." He said. "There's no way I'm going to slow things down now. With the press already smelling something up and with the volatility of the situation over there we need to press on with the mission. I was hoping we'd get some real money to offer for your guys, but obviously Washington won't play. I've talked to the SECDEF on it and I told him your plan. He isn't pleased, but he understands and basically said he didn't want to know anything else. I think they call that 'plausible deniability.'"

"What about this demand to bring out the captain and his family and father?" I asked.

"That's another tough one. It would take days to get permission to do that if I ask. We don't have days." He replied. "Tell you what, there's plenty of room on the C-130, so if your friend can have his family where everyone is grouped together when it's time to climb aboard, fine. But we're not going to get into a tangle with the Iranian Army about it. And we're sure not going to kidnap an Iranian Air Force general if he doesn't want to come along. It will be all up to your buddy."

"OK. I got it. I'll pass the word on to him once I get there. We'll check in with you after we land for any updates."

CHAPTER TWENTY SEVEN

WASHINGTON

Detective Sergeant Welch was very thorough. He interviewed the desk clerks, the maids, the valet parking attendants of the Mayflower Hotel, and he reviewed what there was of security cameras. Back then security cameras were not such a big deal, although after the Watergate affair they became more popular. The only cameras "on duty" at the Mayflower were in the parking garage and one showing a view of the front desk. All of the staff knew Marianne Rodgers and they admitted seeing her with different men over the last few weeks. But no one could (or would) identify anyone specifically. The cameras showed her getting out of her car the night before, alone.

Welch's next stop was the bar at the hotel. The desk clerk had mentioned that Ms. Rodgers frequented the bar just about every night. After questioning a couple of waitresses, Welch made it around to Ricky the bartender. It was obvious Ricky knew something. He was nervous and was constantly looking around. He admitted that Marianne was in the bar the night before, and he admitted she was with a man, though he couldn't identify him.

He pointed out where they were seated and Welch asked if the wait staff that serviced that table was around tonight. He was directed to one of the girls he had just talked to. Because Welch thought Ricky was hiding something, he asked the girl to approach them there at the bar.

"Miss, I'm told you served Marianne Rodgers and a man there at that table last night. Is that right?" Welch asked.

"Oh yeah!" she said as if surprised. "I guess I did."

"Do you know the man? Can you describe him?"

"Well, actually there were two men. She came in with one of them and they sat down there, then this other guy came over and started yelling at them." She described. "You remember don't you Ricky? You had to break up a fight between 'em." She directed at the bartender.

Ricky looked perplexed, but finally came through. "Yeah, I remember. It was about to get ugly and I told the one guy to leave. He did, but not without making a scene."

"So Ricky, do you know who these guys were? Do they come in here a lot? Can you describe them?" Welch pursued.

Ricky hemmed and hawed, and finally said "Do I need a lawyer here? Am I gonna get drawn into court?"

"Geesh Ricky. I don't know. Did you do something wrong? Why do you think you might need a lawyer?" Welch queried.

"Because of who this one guy is." Ricky sheepishly answered. "He's a pretty big cheese around here."

"Tell me who we're talking about Ricky. You can either do it here or we can go down to the station. If you think you need a lawyer, you can call one to meet you there. If you're afraid of this guy, I can only say we can put you in protective custody until we get him off the streets. Now who are we talking about." Welch persisted.

"I don't know who the guy she came in with was, and I do know he hightailed it out the back when I separated the two of them." Ricky was getting around to it. "But the one guy is Bobby Taggart, I think he's the President's Chief of Staff. He's in here a lot, especially lately."

Duke Welch knew this was about to get way above his pay grade. He interrogated Ricky a little farther and found out that Taggart had met Marianne at the bar here two nights ago and they left together - he figured they were going up to her room. They were playing all "lovey dovey" before leaving. Welch left then and went straight to the station house to talk to his boss. He knew that there were some things the President and his staff couldn't be touched for, but he didn't think murder or even knowledge of a suicide were among them. He also knew he'd better run it all up his chain before pursuing Taggart any further.

Back at the Mayflower, another Washington Post reporter had been snooping around. He was seated at the bar down a bit from where Detective Welch was interrogating Ricky and the waitress. He couldn't hear anything, but he could guess that they were talking about Marianne's "suicide." He was Peter Sciapini, and he didn't believe for a minute that Marianne Rodgers, queen of all the bitches, would off herself. She was too fucking ornery and too high on herself. Peter wouldn't miss her much and in fact, with her gone, he might be able to move up a notch in the pecking order of the Washington Post's reporter ladder. He smelled a big story here. First he approached the waitress and tried to sweet talk her into information. All he got though was that there were two guys making a fuss over Rodgers. She had seen one of them before, but she couldn't (or wouldn't) give him a name. So then "Ski Pee" went to the bar and ordered a beer from Ricky.

"So Ricky, I saw you talking to that cop earlier. Do you have any information about Marianne Rodgers and her death? Who were the guys she was in here with last night."

"I already told that detective all I know and I'm keeping my nose out of it now." Ricky retorted.

"But you do know who they were, right?" Peter pushed .

"Like I said, I've SAID all I'm gonna say. There's too much political bullshit attached to this issue." Ricky answered.

"What do you mean 'political bullshit'? Were these guys politicians?" Ski Pee leaned in close and slipped a hundred dollar bill across the bar. "Help me out here Ricky. I promise I'll keep your name out of it."

Ricky looked at the money for a few seconds, looked around to be sure no one was watching, and then palmed the bill into his pocket. "Ok. You didn't hear it from me right? But the guy who caused all the ruckus in here last night was the same guy Ms. Rodgers took up to her room the night before."

"And?" Ski Pee prodded.

"It was Bobby Taggart, President Carver's right hand man.

After picking himself up off the floor, Sciapini smiled a big one and said "Thanks Ricky. I'll remember you for this one." as he headed for the door.

"No! I'd rather you forget you ever saw me." Ricky hollered after him.

Bobby Taggart didn't show up for work Wednesday morning. He didn't answer phone calls from others in the White House staff. One of the senior staff members tried to fill in for him in attending to the President's needs, but Carver too was wondering where his trusted aide was. One of the duties Taggart always attended to every morning was to arrange the newspapers for his boss and he would highlight the articles Bobby thought Carver should for sure read. The headline in the Washington Post was not highlighted, but it didn't have to be. It took up half the page.

"White House Chief of Staff Implicated in Post Reporter's Death" The story went on with Peter Sciapini's byline that Taggart was being investigated by the D.C. police who apparently believe Marianne Rodger's death was not a suicide. It described the second hand information about the events of the night before, and more importantly the night before Rodgers filed her story about a pending conflict with Iran. It went on to dive deeper into the report of a hostage rescue mission about to go down in southern Iran. Basically all Sciapini did was repeat the allegations Rodgers had made in her story and then added enough sensationalism to it to lead one to believe Taggart murdered Rodgers because she printed the information she had squeezed out of him in bed the night before.

CIA Director Durkee demanded an immediate audience with the President. He was admitted into the White House kitchen where Carver was chowing down on grits and eggs and glancing at the newspapers.

"Mr. President, I see you've read the Washington Post article? Do you have any idea where Mr. Taggart is? On second thought, never mind that sir. We've got a bigger problem now." Durkee blurted out.

"Sit Down Dick. Ya want some breakfast? The chef here makes a great down home southern Virginia ham and eggs — and grits of course." The President answered. " No I don't know where Bobby is. It sounds like though he'd better be hiding under a rock someplace."

"Yes sir, but like I said, we have a bigger issue. This article here tells the Iranians everything but the timeline of our pending action. I'm afraid we may be putting a lot more Americans in harms way. Trouble is, I don't think we can stop it at this point. The C-130 with the engine is on its way. I'm thinking we'd better just try to get word to them to drop off the engine, load up all our people and get out of dodge. We can just leave the aircraft there for them." Durkee explained.

"If I'm not mistaken, that's about what I said the other day when y'all started talkin' about ransom money." Carver countered. "Just press on and do what you think is best Dick. Hopefully these hotheads in Tehran will leave it all alone."

Durkee left the White House and went directly to the Pentagon. He collected Admiral Miller and General Furman along the way and they convened in the Joint Chief's Command Center. It took almost an hour, but they were finally able to connect with Speedball in Dhahran. Their fears were substantiated. It was already pushing dusk in Iran and Saudi Arabia. The C-130 was probably already on the ground at Shiraz and the HH-53s were just about too launch for their night intrusion into southern Iran with the UDTs on board. Speedball did inform Durkee of Mitchell's grand scheme faking a ransom payment and about the Iranian family that wanted to defect. After a few "You Gotta Be Shittin' Me" and "Jesus Christ" comments it was decided to just sit back and keep their fingers crossed. There simply were not any communication lines open to anyone in Shiraz.

CHAPTER TWENTY EIGHT

SHIRAZ

We were 20 miles out on our descent into Shiraz. I had familiarized the Tango Team members the best I could with the engine we were about to unload. Not that I was an expert by any means on transporting and manhandling a couple thousand pound Pratt & Whitney J-79 engine. But at least I knew what it looked like and have seen them sitting on the big aluminum "carts" they ship them in. These guys were to masquerade as Air Force enlisted men tasked with unloading the cargo. Then the plan was for the lot of us to kind of "melt" into the crowd with the other 14 airmen in the Tent City. Hahn's engine maintenance specialists would make the swap out and we would hopefully all launch off tomorrow - them in the C-130 and me in the Phantom. Just in case there were any problems, the Tango folks had stashed all their weapons and even some explosive devices in and around the engine. The plan was to unload it, roll it into one of the big tents, remove all the weapons and "foreign objects," and then roll it out tomorrow for the swap out.

About 10 miles out the Loadmaster told me the pilots wanted to see me in the cockpit. I went up and settled into a center jump seat between the two of them. "Captain, we got a problem." Said Lt. Colonel Jack Frye, the aircraft commander. "The tower just told us to land, taxi directly to our parking area and to download our cargo. But we are not to shut down. We're supposed to take off again immediately and leave the country. I asked if we are supposed to load up with passengers and they said 'absolutely not'."

"Shit!" I exclaimed. "They must have figured out what we're doing. Ok. Tell you what. Do what they say and we will quickly unload the engine and roll it inside. Then I'll send out five guys dressed like us to get back on. Hopefully they'll let you take off with the same number of folks you brought in. We're going to need these four guys you got in the back here, but there's likely a few on the ground that we can swap out." I went back to the cargo compartment and strapped in next to Grubman and told them all the change in plans. Obviously it meant the helicopters are going to be our only ticket out. Then I pulled out my "brick" and tried to contact Speedball back in Dhahran. No luck. I got Jani on the phone part of the device though.

"Jani, what's going on? The tower has told this C-130 it has to turn around and leave immediately after off loading the engine. What's happening?" I asked.

"Your newspaper story is what has happened." He answered. "The story says the US is coming to rescue these airmen that it calls hostages. The leaders in Tehran are furious. General Rashid has ordered the C-130 to depart. I will try to talk to you after you land."

The landing was uneventful. The pilot taxied to a spot where there were actually Hahn types to direct him in, and where the area didn't look too crowded with Iranian cops or military. We were able to download the engine like we hoped and rolled it into the larger maintenance tent. While Grubman and his team went about downloading their weapons and explosives I gathered the 14 "hostages" together. The captain who had been left in charge identified five guys to sneak out. Actually it was four guys and one woman. One of the avionics maintenance types was a senior airman woman. She had been having a rough time, especially when out amongst the Iranians. The rest of the group had been very protective of her and accompanied her everywhere, but it was still tough for her. One of the other men was sick with a bad cold and it was feared he would contaminate the rest of the group, so they had isolated him in one of the other tents. This way we could at least keep everyone together - safety in numbers.

Four of the "new passengers" swapped outer jackets with the Tango team who had flight jackets from the Arkansas National Guard. Since I was in a flight suit I gave my flight jacket to the fifth about to be "stowaway." They all moved quickly but not at a run so as to alert the Iranians and they scooted up the ramp of the C-130. The Loadmaster closed up the clamshell doors and it taxied away. A few minutes later the hoped for getaway ride lumbered off into the air heading south. Fortunately the aircraft had enough fuel for a round trip, so if they made it out of Iranian airspace, they should be scott free.

I suggested to Grubman to get Speedball on the horn. The scenario had just changed and we needed to know the plan. In the meantime, I called Jani again. He actually was able to drive down to meet up.

Jani brought a copy of the Tehran English Newspaper that we used to get everyday when we were there for our six weeks. It was basically the Washington Post story outlining the "rumor" that the US was going to come rescue its "hostages." Evidently the Ayatollah and leadership in Tehran had turned the whole thing over to General Rashid with the orders to keep the Americans on base until they decided what to do with us. Jani said Rashid was in a bad mood, probably because he saw his $14 million payday go by the wayside. Well, at least I was off the hook for that one. I'm still not sure how my whole scheme would have gone over with Washington even if I was able to pull off the bluff.

"Have you been able to see your father?" I asked Jani. "Does he know about your plan?"

"Yes and I was surprised that he didn't completely throw me out of his office." Jani responded. "At first he was very mad at me, but he agreed that it was best for our family to flee to the west. Evidently my mother and grandmother, as well as an aunt and two nephews escaped last night by sea. Father even said he would 'think about' going with us, but he did not say he would."

"Well, obviously things have changed." I was not about to tell him we would be raiding the place with a UDT team and two helicopters tomorrow night. I like Jani and I sort of trusted him, but not enough to lay the whole plan out in front of him. I did cast him a nibble though.

"Why didn't your family go with them." I asked.

"There wasn't room on the boat and besides, I'm depending on you to get them out." He answered. Great! More pressure. Just what I needed.

"My instructions were to give you and your family and father a ride out but not to do anything to help you. We cannot be involved in any kind of activity that could be construed as kidnapping. You would have to show up here ready to go." I explained.

"How will you get out now without the C-130?" He asked.

"Good point. I don't know, but I would keep my bags packed if I were you." I said.

CHAPTER TWENTY NINE
SHIRAZ

We spent a restless night in Tent City. We had managed to get communications set up with Speedball in Dhahran, who in turn was hooked up with General Bong in Incirlik. Bong was tuned in to the Pentagon, so everyone was up to speed on our situation. The decision was made to launch the helicopters in to pick everyone up an hour after sunset tomorrow night. We figured that I needed to fly the FCF close to that time or all hell would break loose when I didn't return. That meant I had to fly the mission right at sunset. That was no problem for the first part of the flight because it is still plenty light enough for an hour or so to put on my "show," but it also meant I would have to navigate out of the country to Dhahran in the dark with very little in the way of navigational aids.

The escorts of F-4s and F-15s would launch from Dhahran at about sunset as well. We were convinced that the Sabers would for sure be called into action, because we couldn't imagine the Iranians just letting us go when the choppers came in. Along with the aircraft the IAF had at Shiraz, there were two other bases to the southeast and southwest that had significant forces. At Bandar to the southwest, there was the main contingent of F-14 Tomcats, at Gavbandi there were two squadrons of A-4s, older Vietnam era attack jets. The A-4s would not be a huge threat, since they were more offensive machines (ground attack) than defensive, but the F-14s we knew all about, especially armed with their Phoenix missiles. Our guys would have their hands full.

I got with the engine guys and told them to take their time swapping out the engine. They needed to stretch it out so that the jet is ready to fly about 5 PM, but not much before that. Once they quit work, the Iranians would assume we're going to go ahead with the FCF. They apparently had no guidance about what to do with us, satisfied to just let us mill around, yet definitely confined to our quarters. I conferred with Grubman and the other Tango folks. They decided to wire the explosives up to cover the side of Tent City that faces the rest of the base, figuring that if the Iranians decided to move in on us, they would come from that direction. "Stinker" handled that part of the operation while "Longshot" set himself up at a strategic position to cover the approach with his long rifle, hoping to pick a few of the attackers off as they moved in.

Thursday morning I went out to the jet with the engine maintenance guys and the spare engine. We had more folks than we needed to push the big cart the J-79 was cradled in, but no one else needed to know that. I was surprised to see that there were no Iranian guards on the airplane. They had pulled back away from it and from the entrance to Tent City. I did see though that there was a lot of activity around the IAF aircraft. It appeared they were prepping their jets to fly. About that time my "brick" rang. It was Jani.

"Brad, when will you fly your mission?" He asked.

"It probably won't be until later this afternoon, they are having some problems. I guess the new engine doesn't have all its parts, so they are taking them from the old one." I lied.

"What's going on with you guys? Are you flying today."

"I don't think so. We are just keeping busy." He lied back. Since it looked to me like they were loading live missiles on the F-4s, that seemed more than just busy work.

"Have you heard anything from your father?" I asked.

"Not since yesterday. Do you have anything arranged to leave the country?" He was fishing.

"Not yet. But if we do anything you will have to move fast if you still want to leave with us." I sort of lied again.

"I won't be going anywhere." He said. "I am on the schedule to fly in an alert status, but Brad - I have to ask you. If you do go, please take my wife Doria and the children with you."

"Without you?"

"Yes. I want them to have a better life, and I will try to join them later. Maybe with my father as well." Jani sounded desperate.

"I can't promise anything, but if something comes up you will have to get them down here." I didn't really think it would work, but there would be room on the HH-53s. They each will carry 38 troops. Since there were 15 of us total, and eight Tangos and UDTs aboard, there would still be room.

"Ok. Brad, thank you. I hope somehow this all works out and you and your countrymen get out. Hopefully we will meet again someday." He sounded dejected.

The engine swap was done by about one PM. The maintenance folks spent the next 4 hours tinkering, cleaning, doing their best to keep busy. In the meantime, Grubman organized the group to position themselves near the back of the complex. Those that could be were armed. All documents and anything valuable, but not valuable enough to take with us, was piled up near the front. The explosives were wired and Stinker had a detonation charge that he would toss into the fray at the right time. At five o'clock I stepped to the jet with my gear.

I pre-flighted the Phantom and then went up to strap down the back seat. I turned the radar on since the crew chief had external power applied, I turned on the inertial nav system as well. One big problem already. The INS would not come on. Then I remembered that the nav set was swapped out with the bird that aborted from the launch on Sunday. That one was on the ramp in Dhahran. *Great! I won't even have a platform displayed. I definitely would be flying "by the seat of my pants" on this sortie. And at night too!* At least the weather was good. So long as that held up I should be ok. Hopefully I will be able to find Dhahran. I remembered that there should be two F-15s up there dedicated to escorting me home. All fine and dandy as long as they don't have to peel off to chase a bad guy.

I started the jet up and ran through the checks. Then came the first test.

"Shiraz ground control, Saber 61 ready for taxi for test flight." There was a long pause. I tried again. "Shiraz ground Saber 61?"

Evidently the tower personnel had to check with someone with a higher pay grade, but finally "Saber 61, you are cleared to taxi to Runway Zero One, altimeter 30.12."

I acknowledged the altimeter setting, set my altimeter and gave the pull-the-chocks signal to the crew chief. He did so and the lot of them left from the flight line and hustled into Tent City.

I taxied out to the runway, did my pre-takeoff checks and switched to tower control. "Shiraz Tower, Saber 61 ready for takeoff, request VFR departure. I will remain in the local area." This was the second time in a week I made a bogus takeoff from Shiraz. At least this time though, they cleared me and my radio didn't mysteriously break down.

"Saber 61 Tower, cleared for takeoff, you have no traffic in the area." I hoped that wasn't true. There should be a couple of helicopters inbound, down in the dirt.

I took the runway, pushed the power up to full military (full power without the afterburners) and checked the gages over carefully. After all this **was** a real FCF and I wanted to be sure the new engine acted correctly. I released the breaks and went to full AB, got the familiar soft kick in the pants and launched off into the dusk. As I lifted off, I glanced down at the IAF ramp. It looked like several of their jets were running and four had just started taxiing out. *Aw shit! They must know something's up.* After I climbed above about 5000 feet and away from the Shiraz control zone I switched my radio over to the pre-briefed frequency for the choppers.

"Jolly 01, Grizzly. Jolly 01, Grizzly, come in." I called for the rescue folks.

"Grizzly, this is Jolly. We're airborne and inbound."

"Roger Jolly. What's your ETA?" I needed to know how to time my diversional fly over.

"We should cross the perimeter fence in 9 minutes."

Wop responded.

"Roger that. Be advised the IAF squadron is in the process of launching their jets and they are armed. They obviously either know or suspect something is up. Do you have comm with Dhahran?" I asked.

"Roger Grizzly. We have them on HF (High Frequency Radio)." Wop came back.

"Ok. Suggest you contact them and/or the cavalry and send them in. I think it's going to get pretty hot here for you and our folks on the ground." I wanted them to get the Sabers and the Eagles headed inbound, even though we didn't know for sure the IAF launch was because of us or not.

"Can do Grizzly. Good luck on your end." She answered.

"Thanks. You too. Ok, I'm going back to the tower freq to shine my ass." I signed off and switched over to tower just in time to hear them clear 'Gordo Flight' of four F-4s for takeoff.

I put my steed into a steep dive and pushed the power up to full military. I had about 450 knots when I crossed over the base at about 500 feet, zoomed up into a climb and selected full afterburner. Looking down I saw four more IAF jets nearing the runway. I sliced back down and this time I was doing over 600 knots when I crossed the base proper. I was doing very close if not over the Mach, and I could just imagine the windows blowing out of a few buildings. That should get their attention. It definitely got the attention of the folks in the tower.

"Saber 61, you are to discontinue your flight and return to base immediately." They squawked at me.

"Roger Tower, lining up for a straight in, full stop now." I lied again. I was lining up for a straight in approach, and I had my landing gear hanging, and as I approached about three miles out I could see two large helicopters crossing the opposite perimeter of the base and settle down by our Tent City area.

I got to the end of the runway, raised the gear and flaps, selected full AB again and climbed out to the south. I put my head on a swivel looking for Jani's squadron mates and switched my radio back to our pre-briefed "rescue frequency."

"This is Grizzly in the blind. Airborne and heading to the nest. Any mother hens out there?" I was looking for some Eagles.

"Grizzly, this is Saber One. We're inbound with eight." It was Lt. Colonel Watson. "Any action for us back there?"

"Roger sir. They got at least 8 of their F-4s airborne and our choppers are on the ground likely picking up more than passengers. They can probably use your help." I replied.

"Copy that. The Eagles are out here somewhere to give you a hand. Sabers go to attack freq." He switched his guys over to the frequency that should allow him to talk to Grubman or at least the choppers.

"Grizzly, this is Shogun. Got you loud and clear and hopefully a buddy lock." That was an F-15 pilot. "Buddy Lock" meant that if my radar warning device was picking up a detection, it could be him. I had a detection from the right one o'clock area, but I also had one from my six.

"Roger Shogun, Grizzly's got two hits, one from my six."

"That's not us but we see him, keep coming. We should be about on your nose for 6 miles." That voice was familiar.

"Copy that. Is this Silo?" I asked. Silo is the tactical call sign the Bitburg guys gave to Pete Trask since he had come from his last assignment as a missile control officer. A "Silo" is what the missiles are housed in out in the boondocks.

"Roger that Griz. Here to bail you out of trouble …. again."

CHAPTER THIRTY

FIREFIGHT

The HH-53s came in very low, so low they were kicking up all kinds of dust and sand. They sat down as close as they could to the tents and the UDTs deployed immediately. They set up a perimeter of about hundred yards and Grubman started shooing the airmen out of the tents. The Iranian army guards came in hot and strong. They had trucks with 50 caliber machine guns mounted in the back and plenty of firepower. Longshot was able to pick off several of the rag heads before they could get within range of their own weapons. Deadeye was with the UDTs and she too did some damage. She was about to take out the driver of what looked to be a Land Rover when it stopped and a woman got out. She scrambled to the back door of her car and pulled two children out and started running toward the tents. A jeep pulled up behind her Land Rover and two Iranian army guys got out. One of them pulled out a sniper rifle of his own and looked to be aiming at the fleeing woman with her children. Deadeye didn't know anything about Jani's wife maybe joining them for the ride, but she didn't like the looks of this. Two quick shots and both Iranians were on the ground with half their heads missing. I had told Grubman about the potential stowaways, but neither of us believed it would come to anything and he had not spread the word amongst his people. Deadeye moved in and intercepted Jani's wife and pulled them all under cover. She called Grubman on the radio.

"Grub, I've got a woman and a couple kids here. She says they want a ride. What guidance?"

"Oh shit!" Grubman said. "Ok bring 'em with you. I think they're ok, but check her for explosives." Grubman was familiar with some radicals using women with explosive vests as suicide killers. Deadeye checked the three of them over and sent them on with the contingent of Hahn folks. They all got on board the first HH-53 and the UDTs and Tango started pulling the perimeter in tighter.

Stinker stayed back toward the tents. As the first wave of Iranians hit the Tent City he tossed in his detonator. The place went up in a huge explosion of fire and death. Just then the first flight of Sabers came roaring across at a couple hundred feet. They laid down CBU in a pattern starting with the tents and for a hundred yards towards the base proper. Troops, jeeps, trucks and buildings all went up in flames. The HH-53s lifted off just as a second wave of fighters blew over. Lt. Colonel Watson and his flight came back around for one last pass and spread bomblets all through the IAF F-4 parking area. The remaining jets on the ground and most of their equipment went up in flames. Then the Sabers headed south, staying low, looking for airborne threats.

I picked up Silo and his flight of four as they passed over top of me in a steep banked turn. He cleared his second element off to catch up to the Sabers in case they needed any help. It turns out the threat that was at my six o'clock was one of Jani's squadron F-4s. It was by itself which was unusual, although I didn't know that at the time. He was doing the speed of snot and was catching up. Silo and his number two Eagle saw him coming and converted to the Iranian's six o'clock. Just as they were about to blow his shit away the F-4 pilot started rocking his wings. "Grizzly. This guy's got something funny up his sleeve," Pete said. He's back here at your six just rocking his wings. I immediately thought of Jani. Could it be him trying to defect?

"Copy. It could be a defection. I'm going to give the rejoin signal and start an easy turn. Let's see what he does." I rocked my wings dramatically, the universal rejoin signal, then I rolled into a 30 degree turn to the left. The Iranian pulled his nose out in front and basically matched my bank angle, starting to slide into a position on my wing. A rather gruff, deep voice came up on the emergency guard radio frequency with "American F-4 over the coast in left hand turn, this is Gordo 3, request permission to come aboard." the voice was not Jani's. I was confused.

"Gordo three come up 301.0." I said to get him off the emergency frequency.

"Three."

"Shogun copies." Trask wanted to hear us too.

I checked all of us in on the frequency and said, "Gordo 3 identify yourself and state intentions."

The gruff voice came back. "I am Major General Masur Ranjahni. I am requesting asylum for myself and my son. he is in my back seat."

"Copy that sir. Welcome aboard. Maintain a loose route formation. I will probably need to give you the lead. I have no inertial navigation and only minimum flight instruments. We are headed for Dhahran Air Base, Saudi Arabia." I was losing the horizon now as it got darker.

"Roger Grizzly. We can take the lead at your discretion." The general responded.

"Grizzly. Shogun's going to maintain an outrigger formation. Let me know if you need any help." Trask was little leery of all of this 'diplomacy'."

We were just crossing the Iranian coast outbound at about 15,000 feet and climbing. We were about 110 miles from Dhahran.

"Shogun Two has two bogeys left eight o'clock high, three miles." It was still light enough at 15,000 feet for visual contacts. I snapped my head over that way just in time to see a missile come off the wing of one of the attackers. Pete saw it too.

"Shoguns, Grizzly, break left. Incoming!"

The Ranjahnis were on my left side, looking right to fly formation on me. They broke as well, but a little late and climbed and slid to the outside of my turn. Halfway through the turn the missile blew up with a proximity fuse underneath the Iranian F-4. They were splattered with missile shrapnel and fireball.

I kept the turn going to defeat the attacker, but Pete and his wingman had them sandwiched. They were two F-14s flying in basically a fingertip formation - maybe a little looser, and boring straight in for their target - my new wingman. I lit the afterburners and took it up to a nose high yo-yo (high angle climbing turn reversal) to pick up the F-4 wallowing in a right hand turn - obviously seriously damaged.

"Fox Two, Fox Two." Both Pete and his wingman let loose with heat seekers that found their targets and both F-14s exploded. One was a tremendous blast. The missile must have hit the fuel tanks. The other sheered off one wing of the Tomcat and the jet tumbled into a spin.

I leveled off my hard turn and put the F-4 in my windscreen. It was wallowing severely and after a few seconds, "Mayday, Mayday. Gordo bailing out." Then there were two ejections and two good chutes.

"Shogun, Grizzly - can you stick with them? See where they land? I need to head for the house. I'm sucking fumes." I asked Pete to try and determine where Jani and his father land so that we might be able to pick them up.

"Roger. Shogun Two, escort this wounded puppy back to Dhahran. I'll stick around here. The choppers should be coming by shortly." I hadn't thought of that. Our Jollys should be approaching the coast outbound within the next half hour. At that point I didn't have time to think about anything else. I needed to get my jet on the ground. I was looking at about 15 minutes of flying time left. I gave Shogun Two the lead and he led me back to Dhahran for an uneventful landing. I turned the jet over to our guys from Hahn who had come in on a C-141 a few hours ago and I went to find Speedball.

Meanwhile, back at the OK Corral, half of Shiraz was on fire, our choppers were hugging the earth and heading south as fast as they could, the Sabers had joined up and were also pressing south at low level with two F-15s escorting, and the other four Eagles flying a cap over the choppers at about 5000 feet. The Iranian F-4s were floundering. Two of them tried to intercept one of the Sabers after his attack on the base, but when the American F-4 dove down in the dirt they didn't follow and lost him. They were basically flying around in a loose fingertip formation like they had never learned any other way.

Another flight of Iranian F-4s managed to get lucky. They had radar contact with the F-15s at 5000 feet. Actually that probably wasn't very lucky. The Eagles saw them at about the same time, took it straight up into the vertical and then pulled hard to the rag heads' six o'clock. It was a classic repositioning maneuver that the F-4s couldn't, or wouldn't attempt to match. It was almost completely dark and they were too low for comfort. They got a lot lower in a few seconds though. One of them took an AIM-7 radar guided missile in the snout and the other took an AIM-9 heat seeker up the ying yang.

It was almost over. Almost. As they approached the coast, Colonel Watson and his flight started an easy climb assuming there would be no more rocks to hide them. Unfortunately that was a mistake. Two F-14s were about 20 miles off shore in a high orbit. They were two more of the same flight Pete and I had tangled with. They saw the F-4s climb out of the ground clutter and fired off a Phoenix missile each. Watson caught the radar warning alert and called for a hard turn to put the missile on the beam and chaff. Unfortunately the chaff dispenser on Saber three's jet malfunctioned. That was Major Shivner (the 'loaner' pilot from Incirlik) and Rhino - my GIB. They rolled out of the turn as the missile hit and blew the tail off the jet. They ejected at about 5000 feet over a small island just off the coast near the Iranian town of Dovner.

Trask followed the general and his son down in the silk and initialized his inertial nav to mark the spot. Then he climbed up to about 5000 feet and tried to contact Jolly 01. It almost became a real goat rope there because he was out over the coast at the same altitude his squadron mates were as they escorted the choppers, and the Hahn F-4s were climbing out in the same general area. There were a few tense moments as everyone had targets on the radar, not knowing if there were anymore bad guys out there. They straightened it out though and Pete was able to pass coordinates to Wop and Red Baron in the choppers. Jani had not silenced his emergency locator beacon and Wop was able to home in on it. She swooped in, picked up the two Iranian pilots, and headed out to sea. Not knowing who they were though, the UDTs kept a close watch on their new passengers. Jani's wife and kids were in the other chopper, so Jani did not know they had made it out until he got to Dhahran.

CHAPTER THIRTY ONE

RESCUE

Shivner and Rhino landed on the small island. There were not any lights on anywhere, so they thought it might be uninhabited, but took no chances. Shivner severely strained his back in the ejection, so he could barely move, but they managed to gather up their chutes, turn off their locator beacons, and Rhino came up on Guard frequency.

"Mayday, Mayday, this is Saber 3 Bravo, looking for a ride." He broadcast in the blind. The F-15s were the last to land back at Dhahran and one of the pilots heard the call. He broke out of his landing approach and zoomed to higher altitude to get better reception.

"Saber 3 Bravo, Shogun one one, come up channel alpha." The Eagle driver directed Rhino off the main channel that everyone in the air (including the bad guys) was on.

They connected on one of the other channels and it was determined that the entire force was on the ground or about to be, and in no shape to go back for a pick up. Shogun suggested Rhino go off the air and come back up in two hours. It would take that long to launch any kind of search and rescue force and there was no use draining his radio battery. Rhino agreed, shut down and went about hiding and administering what aid he could to his front seater. He did manage to pass on however that they had landed on a small island and he was able to give a pretty accurate description of where it was. After all, he was a navigator by profession, and one of the best at that. He kept track of where they were all through any flight. I had relied on Rhino on many a sortie to keep us on the right track and bring us home.

Both Colonel Watson and the eagle driver called in to operations to alert everyone of the downed crew. I immediately got with Tony Gilford and Pete Trask to try and put together a rescue operation as soon as we could. I knew that the Iranian navy was all over the gulf, still there from the big exercise we ran on them last week, and probably re-energized with the intel that we might be mounting a raid on Shiraz. The Saudi Air Force was very helpful. Their intel folks confirmed that there were several Iranian ships in the area of that island, after all, it was within Iran's maritime boundary. They said there were also a lot of fast gunboats in the area near the ports of Dovner and Kangka.

Unfortunately we had used all the CBU we brought with us and the Saudi's weren't able to rearm us. Same thing with the missiles the F-15s used. However, not all eight of them fired their missiles. Pete was able to scramble together four jets and identified three wingmen to fly with him out front on any rescue escort mission. We also were able to move air to air missiles around to have four F-4s armed, but the only air to ground munitions we had were the high explosive rounds in our guns. We were strafe only when it came to an attack scenario.

As soon as Colonel Watson came in from his flight I jumped on him to ask to lead the mission. At first he resisted, wanting to lead the flight himself, but I pleaded with him that Rhino was my GIB and I wanted to try to get him out. I convinced him that he should stay in the Saudi command post to coordinate everything. Speedball was an organized and proven leader, but he had no experience in coordinating an air rescue. Watson gave in and I picked Boomer and Bosco as my numbers two and four, and Scotty "Beam Me Up" Perkins as number three and deputy lead. All we needed now was a helicopter.

Wop and Red Baron were about halfway across the gulf when they heard the chatter on the radio about another downed crew. They were too low on fuel to go back and came into Dhahran as quick as they could. We got fuel to them as fast as we could move the Saudi ground crews. We also got the 4 F-4s and 4 F-15s gassed up and armed within about an hour of their landing.

We got everyone in a conference room near the Saudi command center - Colonel Watson, Pete Trask, Wop, Red Baron, me and Speedball. Tony Gilford was tasked to ride heard on the maintenance folks to get the jets and choppers ready. We were shooting for a ten PM take off, an hour twenty from now. Wop decided she would fly the Jolly. Evidently Baron's chopper had taken a few hits of ground fire when he lifted off from Shiraz and he was leaking fuel. Trask would lead his eagles in the same sort of chopper escort scenario as they had practiced before - offset the Jolly so as not to highlight her, but close enough to respond to any threat. The eagle has a gun too, so if it came in as a surface threat they would be just as effective as we would in our guns only Phantoms. I would lead the Sabers off last and blow by Wop and her escort and head directly toward the island. The plan was to blow over the island low enough to wake Rhino up (as if he would be asleep?) and get him on the radio. Then we would set up an orbit north south along the coast just north of the island, ready to pounce on any surface threat, sea or land. We broke up the meeting and went to brief our flights, to be ready to step to the jets in 40 minutes.

Jani and his father were reunited with Jani's wife and kids on the ramp after the choppers landed. The general's wife and the rest of the family were still in custody. The Saudis were not very enamored with having an Iranian two star defector in their midst, but we were able to convince them to drive and "escort" them to Riyadh and the American Embassy there. At that point they would turn them over to the embassy staff and they could file for asylum. That's the last I saw of Jani and his family until much later in the States.

Wop lifted off first. She had Gronk, her own co-pilot, and Snoopy, the other co-pilot with her, and also Squid, one of the Tangos. He had been an Air Force PJ before jumping ship to the Navy and UDT training. She kept it low crossing the Gulf. She could see a few of the ships as she went by, avoiding them and hopefully being invisible to any threats. Pete took off with his four eagles about 15 minutes later and caught up quickly, setting up their northward moving racetrack pattern at 5000 feet, offset to the west of the chopper. I launched off with my four Sabers about ten minutes later. We made formation takeoffs to expedite the join up, and as soon as I was headed north, sent everyone to the briefed formation. Basically we flew two fighting wing formations with Scotty about a half mile back and offset about 40 degrees - close enough he could still see me, but far enough apart to look for bad guys. I kept it down low as well - about 300-500 feet and made a beeline straight for the island. It was dark but there was a good size moon out to help us see each other and miss the water.

I had Fank Gablewski in my back seat. He was a good GIB, although I often wondered how he ever fit back there in "the pit." He was a big guy. He had played linebacker for Bear Bryant at Alabama a couple years before Tom Luck had been there as a tight end. So we called him "Bear," both for his coach, but also because of his size. Bear picked up a couple ships on the radar, so I maneuvered to avoid blowing by them and alerting the forces of evil we were coming. The F-4 radar in the air to ground mode was pretty good in the hands of a good GIB. Over water you could easily detect ships and islands, but you couldn't determine their direction of travel. Also, because the water was pretty rough tonight, it was difficult to detect small targets like gunboats. But Bear did his best and we did see what seemed to be a force of gunboats in a close enough "formation" that they painted pretty well on the radar. They looked to be heading due north toward the island and about 15 miles out. We split them down the middle between our two two ships, Boomer and I on the left, and Scotty and Bosco on the right. One of them confirmed they were gunboats by firing a couple of futile tracer rounds toward the southern two F-4s.

Scotty closed back in on me as we neared the island and we blew across doing about 450 knots. I had switched over to the "alpha" frequency that Rhino had been on earlier and called "Saber 3 Bravo, Saber One One, you up?"

"That's a familiar and welcome voice." He immediately came back. "What'd you think, I was asleep on this tropical isle?"

"Hardly. Break Break, Saber One Three go up common frequency and get the Jolly and Shogun over here." I wanted to get the whole force on the frequency Rhino was on.

"Three." Scotty acknowledged.

"So Bravo, how are you guys?" I queried Rhino.

"I'm fine but the major here really screwed up his back. He can't walk much and can't straighten up when he tries to stand. Nothing protruding, but my guess is a severe sprain or a hip problem."

"Ok. Copy that. Have you seen anyone? Is the island inhabited?" I asked.

"Jolly's up." Wop broke in.

"Shogun check."

"Two"

"Three"

"Four"

"Saber, Shogun's up. Got you in orbit. Some targets farther inland, but no threat so far." Pete checked in his flight.

Rhino broke back in, "I haven't seen anyone. I can see the mainland coast and a few lights, but nothing around here. There is a small temple of some sort built out of rocks, so someone obviously visits once in a while."

"Ok. Saber copies. We'll be orbiting to the north a few miles. Jolly and Shogun, be advised we blew past what looked like a flotilla of gunboats heading this way, probably about 12 miles out by now. No other targets." I switched my attention to the inbound force. "Jolly, we'll be in the briefed orbit. Rescue's over to you."

"Jolly copies." Wop took command of the mission.

"Saber 3 Bravo, Jolly, how do you read me?" She asked Rhino.

"Jolly, you're loud and clear and a sound for sore ears." Rhino came back.

"Roger, I show us about 10 minutes out. Can you describe your position? Which side of the island? Are you under cover? Flat ground or sloped? Do you have any flares?" Wop was trying to get a handle on the environment.

"We're on the northwest side of the island. This thing is just one big rock. Seems to be shaped like a big anvil, at least on this side. We're on the side of it on a pretty good slope. It flattens out down below, but I don't think my pilot can make it down there. He's leaning up against a tree. There are a couple of other trees, but nothing I would call cover. Roger on the flares." Rhino gave a pretty thorough description.

"Copy that. Standby and I'll call for a flare when we're closer. Break Break, Shogun, Jolly's got several wakes up ahead. I'm going to deviate around them to the south." She could tell there were boats out there and didn't want to fly right over them.

"Roger, Shogun's got 'em. Looks to be a half dozen or so on radar."

"Shogun, I think we can call them hostile. One of them took a pot shot at us as we blew by them a bit ago." I jumped in.

"Roger. Shogun three, maintain the orbit looking for air threats. Two, you're with me. Green 'em up guns." Pete was going hunting.

"Two"

"Three copies."

Trask and his wingman made one high speed pass on the gunboats on a diagonal heading across their track. I couldn't see the tracer rounds from my position, but we could see the explosion as one of them blow up. They swept back around and made one more pass - one more definite hit. No telling how many more. The gunboats dispersed and fanned out on their approach to the island. In the meantime, Wop was closing in on the beach.

"Bravo, pop your flare." She ordered. A few seconds later a red flare launched up into the sky from the side of the island.

"Flares away." Rhino called.

"Roger, Visual. Stand by." Wop dropped down lower and hugged the slope of the rock as she approached from the southwest. She blew over Rhino as he was waving a flashlight. "Ok, got your light. Stand by." She cranked the big Huey around and came up from the other side. She went into a hover and then moved around looking for a place to land.

"Ok, Bravo, we're going to have to do this with a hoist. Stand by. Stretcher down first with a PJ." Wop barked out her orders, both to Rhino and to her guys in the back. They hooked up a rescue stretcher to their hoist and Squid slipped on a harness and climbed aboard the stretcher. Gronk pushed the stretcher out the door and they started letting it down. Wop maintained a hover of about 60 feet.

About the time the stretcher hit the ground tracer rounds came blowing in toward the Jolly from the mainland side of the island. We had been monitoring the gunboats coming in from the sea side and didn't see this one who was out in the channel between the island and the coast. The HH-53 has a 50 cal machine gun in the door and Snoopy jumped on it right away, firing back at this new player.

"Uh, Saber, Jolly. We're taking a little heat here. You got this?" Wop said on the radio with all kinds of calm.

Shit, I thought. "Roger that Jolly. Saber one and two are in hot. Three maintain the orbit." I responded. Fortunately Boomer and I were on the inbound leg of our orbit and the gunboat was off to our ten o'clock about four miles. I pushed it up and dove for the source of the tracers, flipped the master arm switch on and squeezed the trigger when I had the boat in sight. Boomer was lighting up the sky beside me and a little behind me as well. We didn't notice any hits but he stopped shooting at the Jolly. I pitched up to avoid the rocky coast and swooped back around for another pass. This put Boomer directly behind me. Fortunately he didn't open fire until after I pulled off, and that meant he was really down there amongst them when he did fire. The gunboat erupted in flames just as Boomer pulled off. He basically flew through the fireball as he honked on the stick for all he was worth to avoid the water and rocks.

"Good shot, Two, but a little close. How're you doing?" I wanted to confirm he didn't take any hits.

"Everything looks ok, but I'm Winchester." He replied. 'Winchester' meant he was out of ammo. So was I.

"Copy that. I'm at your one o'clock 3 miles, cleared to join."

"Visual." He had me in sight. "visual" means you see the good guy, "tally ho" means you see the enemy.

We joined up and then joined Scotty and Bosco in the orbit. In the meantime, Rhino and Squid strapped Shivner into the stretcher and Gronk was bringing him aboard. Gronk pulled the major off and layed him out on the floor of the chopper while Snoopy unhitched the stretcher and hooked up a harness for Rhino. Down went the cable again. In the meantime Wop was holding the Huey straight and level in her hover.

"Three's got two boats coming around the south side of the island. Looks like they're within range to fire soon." Scotty announced.

"Roger three. Cleared hot. One and two are Winchester." Scotty peeled off with Bosco and they blew both the boats out of the water before they could get any shots off at the chopper.

Saber, Shogun, we've got company coming in hot from inland." Pete gave us a heads up. "Looks to be two formations of two in trail. We're engaged." He blew through our orbit in a slight descent and was between us and the incoming.

A minute later, "Shogun's coming hard left for incoming, Three pincer." Pete had detected what had to be a Phoenix missile shot because of the range to the incoming fighters and turned to put it on the beam, pumping chaff. He called for his second element to do the same in the other direction, setting up a pincer attack on the bogeys coming in.

"Three copies."

Rhino climbed into the harness and Squid hooked on beside him. Gronk and Snoopy started reeling them up when even another gunboat opened up on them from the mainland side of the island. "Jolly's taking fire again, right one o'clock." Wop yelled. A little more anxiety in her voice this time.

"Copy Jolly. We're all out of ammo, but in for a high speed pass." I said and dumped the nose and pushed up to full afterburner. Snoopy got on the chopper's 50 cal, but they had to stop reeling in the cable.

Wop had no choice but to get out of the line of fire while letting Snoopy return what he could from her side door. She slowly climbed with Rhino and Squid dangling down below, pulled them clear of the ground and the trees and headed for the beach of the mainland just northwest about two miles. "Saber, I'm heading over to the beach to land and get the chicks aboard." She advised.

"Roger that. Saber Three, give her what cover you can. I responded and continued straight for the gunboat in the channel. "Two are you with me?" I couldn't see Boomer.

"Roger. Two's at your seven o'clock about a mile."

"Ok. Keep me insight but don't come down this low, acknowledge." I didn't want him doing what I was about to do and risk losing two of us. I wasn't really sure what I was going to do anyway without any armament. I thought about jettisoning my wing tanks as I flew over the boat, but I remembered we don't want to do that at 600 knots. Chances are they'll fold right over the wing and crunch! I also had nary a clue about the aerodynamics of the tanks and where to aim. So I decided to just try and scare the living piss out of the rag heads ahead. I leveled off at about

100 feet about a mile in front of the boat. That was lower than I'd ever been at night. But I slowly stepped it down more and more. I didn't dare look inside at my altimeter. I kept all my concentration on the boat and the waves. I did glance up to the mirrors attached to the inside of the canopy bow above the windscreen. What I saw was almost mesmerizing. I was kicking up a spray of water like a rooster tail. I looked back down and now I saw a boat that looked awfully big in my windscreen. It had a couple antennas sticking up to what I was sure was above my altitude. As I crossed over the boat I yanked up on the stick and stuck my tailpipes right in her face. Just before that I witnessed two guys dive overboard. Boomer later told me there were four all together that took a swim, obviously thinking they were about to be rammed.

I pulled out of afterburner, slowed down and pointed back toward the orbit. In the meantime, Wop had reached the coast with her fishing line dangling with its human bait. She set them down gently on the beach, Gronk cut the cable loose and Wop set the Jolly down smoothly beside her chicks. They clamored aboard and she lifted off heading straight for Dhahran. We set up a moving orbit off to the side and followed her on home.

By now the Eagles were kicking some Tomcat ass. The beam maneuver and chaff had defeated the Phoenix and three missiles went blowing by out to sea. When they turned back in they all locked up a different bad guy. The Iranians obviously never (or at least hardly ever) flew at night. Their "formation," (such as it was) was to fly in trail with a couple miles of separation. Obviously no mutual support. Pete basically targeted each of his four eagles on a different F-14. He was able to convert on the leader and lock him up with a good heat source of an AIM-9 missile, and his wingman locked up number two with an AIM-7 radar missile. Two squeezes, two kills. Shogun Three and Four had a little more distance to convert so they both fired their AIM-7s. The lag F-14 took a hit and went down, but the third in line got lucky - for a minute or so. Shogun Three's missile missed, but the idiot Tomcat driver in making his defensive turn to defeat the shot turned his tailpipes right into the Eagle's face. Shogun Three converted to heat seeker and boom! It was all over.

There were more targets out there heading toward the coast but Trask made the right decision and decided to get out of Dodge with us and the Jolly. The eagles caught up to us about half way across the Gulf and set up an outrigger formation on us, keeping our six o'clock covered and clear.

We got everyone on the ground about midnight. There were hugs and handshakes all around, and an ambulance for Major Shivner. He was taken to the Dhahran hospital and flown on an AF C-9 medivac flight to Landstuhl Medical Center in Germany a couple days later. He recovered but he never flew again. His lower three vertebra were basically trashed, and he had to have his back fused. With that, he also walked with a limp, favoring his left hip.

The Saudis were gracious hosts. They brought us to what could only be described as a hotel lounge on the base where they fed us a great meal of steak and all the fixings, but most importantly, all the beer and booze we could ever want. Unusual, since that kind of drinking is supposed to be verboten in Saudi Arabia. We didn't complain and didn't ask.

CHAPTER THIRTY TWO

WASHINGTON

President Carver was concerned about his friend and Chief of Staff Bobby Taggart. Bobby had not been seen or heard from in four days. Detective Welch had interviewed just about everyone on the White House staff, even the President himself. None of the staff had any idea where Taggart was, most didn't care. He was a horse's ass to work for and nobody missed him much. None of them knew of any relationship he may have had with Marianne Rodgers. They knew he was as pissed off as anyone else when her story came out supposedly exposing a U.S. rescue mission in Iran. But since none of them knew anything about the mission anyway, they weren't much help.

The President was even less cooperative. Taggart had been his friend for decades - since high school in southern Virginia. Taggart is the one who convinced Carver to run for Lt. Governor, and when Carver moved up to the Governor's chair he enjoyed the position of Chief of Staff in that role as well. When he convinced Carver to run for President, Taggart ran the campaign. Welch had dug up a few stories of misconduct and indiscretions from back then, but the President denied any knowledge. He simply thought Taggart was a fine upstanding southern gentleman. Welch confirmed in his own mind the President is a weak dick.

Welch and the D.C. police forensics people had been over Taggart's condo with a fine tooth comb. They were admitted to his office as well, but Bobby's deputy and secretary had cleared it of anything that might smack of problems and especially anything that could be classified.

Taggart's car was missing as well. It was a bright red Porsche 911, so it should be easy to spot. That was the only lead that came to any fruition. The car was found on Sunday morning on a deserted stretch of road that dead ends on a spur inlet of the Rappahannock River in Surry County, southern Virginia. Welch hurried down and met up with the county sheriff and the Virginia state troopers. The car was a mess. Taggart was a real slob and there were food wrappers, soft drink cups and cans, lots of finger prints that turned up to be mostly women - hookers that had been arrested and fingerprinted in the D.C. area. There was even a pair of women's underwear behind the passenger seat, and a few used rubbers. A pair of fancy leather driving gloves was found on the driver's seat.

The county called out a search team and a dive operator to search the river in the area. The area was just north of the Scotland-Jamestown Ferry launch site, off County Road 649. In dragging the river immediately in front of where the car was found, a gun was pulled up. It was a 45 automatic with one round fired. A further search found Bobby's body floating amongst a growth of reeds about 200 yards downstream. Preliminary observation showed one gun shot wound to the right temple. Welch thought that a little strange because he had observed during his investigation that Taggart was left handed. Certainly one doesn't have to use his dominant hand to shoot himself, but it wasn't normal in Welch's experience. The Surry County Sheriff took over jurisdiction of the case and had the county coroner transfer the body to their morgue. A full autopsy was performed.

In the meantime, Duke Welch was no further in solving the death of Marianne Rodgers. His main (and only) suspect had been found dead from an apparent suicide. The only other "person of interest" was Major Tom Tyler, Military Assistant to the Secretary of Defense. Welch had interviewed him and he added nothing to the saga of that night at the Mayflower bar. The one interesting thing about it was that he was a married man. When asked about his relationship with Marianne he broke down and said that their date was Marianne's ideas and that she had asked him dozens of questions about the rumor of a pending raid in Iran. Tyler said he refused to answer her questions, but also divulged that he had a late afternoon encounter with Miss Rodgers the same day that she had met with and bedded Bobby Taggart. Tyler swore that he did not discuss any of the pending military action with her, and was extremely nervous about the likelihood the affair would be exposed to his wife. Welch didn't pursue the topic any longer with Tyler, because he was almost certain that because Taggart had disappeared, he was the prime suspect. That is if there was a suspect. It could simply have been that Marianne jumped to her own death.

The next day the sheriff called Welch. "You might wanna come back down here. The coroner's come up with some evidence that makes me think this might not have been a suicide."

"How so?" Welch asked.

"Apparently the victim was smacked on the head hard and likely a couple hours before he was shot." The sheriff explained.

"I'll be there in two hours. In the meantime, can you have your folks go over the car with a fine toothed comb?" Welch asked.

"Already have and that's interesting too. There were plenty of fingerprints in the car, but the steering wheel, gear shift and driver side door handles were clean." The sheriff allowed. "Since when does a guy planning on offing himself wipe down his car on the way? And Taggart's fingerprints were found down by the seat on the passenger side - like maybe he was riding along with his hands down by his side while someone else drove, and that someone wore those driving gloves we found or some other gloves."

"Did you notice any other tire tracks or footprints around the car or on the road?" Welch asked.

"No, but it rained pretty hard last night. I think anything would have been wiped out."

"Ok. I'll call you when I get into town and meet you at the coroner's office." Welch hung up and took off. Before he left he had one of his co-workers check to see if Taggart had a domicile or place in Southern Virginia. "If you have to, ask the President..... or I guess get the Chief to do that."

When he got into Surry, the county seat, Welch stopped by the sheriff's office, and had a message to call his own office. He did so and talked to the detective who had talked to Taggart's assistant.

It appeared Taggart has a cabin on the Rappahannock not far from where the car and the body were found. He mentioned it to the sheriff. "Yeah, I know the place. There used to be some pretty wild parties there. I've had to break them up a couple times, but I don't remember ever seeing Taggart. Usually it was a bunch of teenagers."

"Let's hit the coroner's first and then can you take me out there?" Welch asked.

At the morgue the coroner showed them the body and the apparent wound on the side of the head. "Looks to have been conked by something flat, like maybe a frying pan or the base of a lamp. It's not real obvious - probably why you didn't see it out at the river. And I've discovered this wasn't the 'death blow'" the coroner said.

"But I thought you said he was dead a couple hours before the gunshot wound." Welch queried.

"That's right. Look here." The coroner rolled the body on its side and pointed out a tiny prick of the skin on the side of the right neck. "He was poked with a syringe and shot up with a mixture of formaldehyde and arsenic. That's what killed him. The fact that he'd been dead a while when shot is why there was very little bleeding from the gun shot."

"So," Welch thought out loud. "Mr. Taggart was conked on the head hard enough to probably knock him unconscious somewhere, shot up with a lethal dose of poison, loaded into his own car, driven to the river, shot in the temple, and left for the crabs and jellyfish to mangle. Sheriff, let's get out to that cabin."

Welch followed the sheriff out of town on State highway 31, then north on County Road 649 to a long driveway only two miles from where the car was found. They turned down it and found a small cabin in a scenic spot overlooking the river. There was a dock with a boathouse, a few chairs and picnic tables around, a garbage can with a lid. Welch noticed when he got out of the car some deep ruts in the mud, and a path that ran along the river bank both directions past the dock. He pulled the lid off the garbage can - empty. "When is garbage pick up out here sheriff?"

"Actually it's tomorrow, so this one's been here for 6 days." The sheriff mused.

Did you notice any mud on the side of the Porsche or in the wheel wells? Welch asked.

"No it was pretty squeaky clean on the outside." The sheriff replied.

"Let's go check inside." Welch said.

The cabin was not exactly neat and tidy, but a typical "man cave" with some empty bottles and cans around. But it wasn't trashed either. There was a half empty bottle of Old Grandad on the coffee table with one glass about half full. Nothing indicated more than one person had been in there lately, but it did appear that whoever was drinking bourbon didn't finish it for one reason or another. Welch went over the place thoroughly for about an hour, then he started again, beginning at the front door. The sheriff got bored and after the first hour he was ready to leave.

"I've got a county to police. Ok if I leave you here? Just lock it up on your way out." he said.

"Sure. I'll probably stick around another hour or two. I'll stop by your office on the way out of town if I find anything." Welch replied.

Detective Welch was extremely thorough. He wore gloves as he went through everything - drawers, desk, seat cushions, bedding, dishes, medicine cabinet, book shelves, tool kit, …. Wait! Book shelves. There was a nook in one corner of the main room with three shelves of books. Mostly dime novels and Louis L'amour books. On the bottom shelf, which was really the top to a chest with a couple drawers, there was a bookend holding the books together. But only one bookend. It was a horse's head from the neck up, large and heavy. But the books had fallen over at the other end. No horse. Welch picked up the bookend and inspected it. It had a flat bottom about 6" square. By holding on to the nose of the horse, Welch swung the bookend like a tennis smash. It would make a good weapon, and if connected with a man's head on the flat bottom, would likely knock him unconscious without creating a gaping wound. He looked around the cabin for the second bookend. Nothing. He also found a nightstand drawer that had cloth, some gun cleaning swabs, some gun oil, and a box of 45 caliber shells. No gun.

Welch's last place to look was in the garbage. There was a standard kitchen bin under the sink. It was lined with a plastic bag and was about half full of TV dinner trays, paper napkins, cups, and what looked like leftover lasagna. It didn't smell too bad, so he surmised it wasn't much more than a week old. He poured the contents out on the small kitchen table. Voila! A syringe that had been fully emptied and thrown in the bin. Welsh scooped everything back into the bin except the syringe, looked around one more time, and then left with the bookend and the syringe.

Back in Surry he stopped first at the coroner's office. He was lucky to catch the coroner just before he called it a day. "I found this bookend at the victim's cabin. Could its opposite end be what conked our boy on the head?" He asked the coroner.

"I don't know. Let's take a look." He said and took the bookend while walking back into the morgue. They had stuffed Taggart in a drawer in the refrigerated holding section. The coroner slid the drawer out, uncovered Taggart's upper torso and lifted his head exposing the area of the skull where it had been bashed. He held the bookend up to the area, turned it around a bit, grabbed it by the nose of the horse and made a swinging motion toward the bruised area. "I'd say you've found the knock out weapon detective." He said. "At least one just like it."

"Great! Now, one more thing." Welch said as he pulled the syringe out of his pocket. He had put it in a plastic evidence bag he always carried with him. "Can you analyze this to see what might have been in it, and have your folks check both these for prints?"

"Well, 'my folks' is me this time of day." The coroner snorted. "Everyone else is gone for the day. Since you caught me still here, I guess I can oblige." He took the syringe and the book end to a lab table and got to work.

"Tell you what," Welch said, "I'm gonna head over to the sheriff's office for a bit. Call me there if you get anything."

"Yes sir 'boss.' Should take me about an hour." The coroner supposed.

Welch stopped at the sheriff's office and checked in. He told the sheriff about what he had found, and they sat down to brainstorm the crime. The best guess is that Taggart had escaped the heat of the reporter's death and come down to his cabin to spend a few days and drink his sorrows away. He was sitting on his sofa with a glass of Old Grandad when someone came in and bonked him on the head with the bookend. Since there was no evidence of a struggle, it was likely the perpetrator was hiding in the cabin when Bobby entered. After knocking Taggart unconscious, the killer injected him in the neck with a syringe loaded with enough poison to kill a horse. He threw the syringe in the garbage, looked around in the bedroom and found the gun in the nightstand, scooped Bobby up and put him in the passenger seat of the Porsche, and using the fancy driving gloves in the car, he drove down to the river. He pulled Taggart out, dragged him down to the river, put the 45 automatic to Bobby's right temple and blew his brains out. Then he tossed the gun out into the river and pushed the body off into the stream.

The killer then went back to the car, dropped the gloves on the seat, and hoofed it up the trail to the cabin. There, wearing a pair of his own gloves, like he did when he entered the place the first time, entered the cabin, did a quick sweep, picked up the bookend, and took off, sliding in the mud as he drove out.

"Two questions," Welch said. "Why didn't Bobby see the car parked there when he drove up, and where is the bookend now?"

"What if Bobby didn't drive up?" The sheriff surmised. "What if he was there first and the killer simply snuck up on him? He'd put down a lot of that Old Grandad if the bottle was full when he started drinkin' and he might have dozed off."

"Good point." The phone rang. It was the coroner. He had the results of his work.

"There were no prints on the syringe or on this bookend, but didn't you say it was probably the twin to this horse that did the deed?" The coroner asked.

"Yeah, just thinkin' maybe he handled them both, but it looks like he was wearing gloves anyway." Welch answer, then asked, "What about the syringe? What was in it?"

"You hit the jackpot there. It has traces of formaldehyde and arsenic. In my opinion, this syringe is the murder weapon."

Welch drove back up to his station in D.C. It was almost 11 pm when he got there. He figured he next step would be to talk to Major Tyler again, but there wasn't any hurry. He did some quick paperwork and went home for a few hours of sleep.

CHAPTER THIRTY THREE

DHAHRAN

Most of us basically took the next day off. Those that came in from Shiraz, and especially Rhino needed some rest. The maintenance folks that came down from Germany on the C-141 worked on readying the jets to fly out tomorrow. There was a contingent from Bitburg that had bussed over to Hahn to catch the C-141 when they came down. They worked on the F-15s while the Hahn guys readied their F-4s. Red Baron worked on his chopper as well. He grabbed a couple maintainers to help him, but evidently the HH-53s carry a pretty good "tool box" with them all the time, equipped with a patch kit to plug up bullet holes in the fuel cells. He basically had it repaired by the end of the day, and he and Wop left that night to sneak back through Iraq and Syria to Incirlik, Turkey. A Navy chopper came in and scooped up the UDTs and took them out to the USS Enterprise.

The Arkansas Guard C-130 left as well. They were overdue returning to the states and they were looking forward to getting home to some good home cookin.' They took Speedball and the other Tango team members with them and went in to Incirlik.

The rest of us - the aircrews from Hahn and the pilots from Bitburg lolled around one of Dhahran's nicer hotels. The Saudis were gracious hosts, but it was obvious they wanted us out as soon as possible. They kept offering all kinds of help to hasten our departure.

Pete Trask and his Bitburgers launched off about 1000 hours Sunday morning. We took off an hour later. All of us went into Incirlik with the expectation of turning and hopping over to Aviano, Italy that afternoon. Our maintainers joined forces and launched off mid afternoon on the C-141 all the way to Hahn. One full aircrew of Sabers rode along too, since we were down one F-4 that Shivner and Rhino had deposited in the Gulf.

The Eagles were able to refuel and fly out to Aviano, but General Bong had other ideas for us, or at least for me and Lt. Colonel Watson. He gathered us and the Tango Team in the Incirlik Command Post shortly after we landed. Pretty soon we were sitting around a table talking to the Secretary of Defense, Chairman of the Joint Chiefs, the Chief of Staff of the Air Force, and the National Security Advisor on a conference call. They basically conducted a mission debrief, and since I had been in on just about every aspect of the mission, it was Speedball and I that did most of the talking. I pretty much ran down the whole saga, stopping once in a while to answer their questions. When I got to the part about offering a monetary payment as ransom I tried to skim over it. SECDEF Malloy wouldn't let it go however. "Where did that cockamamie idea come from? Who determined the amount?"

"Sir, I'm afraid it was my idea." I admitted. Speedball didn't seem in much of a hurry to jump in for my defense. "In my discussions with my Iranian contact and his squadron commander, they led me to believe that simply the exchange of the jet on their ramp for 14 airmen would not appease the general in charge. After all, they already had the F-4. It was on their ramp under their control. The squadron commander knew the general pretty well - at least he thought he did, so he thought the money, deposited directly into the general's hands might work. We obviously figured the general would keep the money and not let anyone up his chain know about it."

"Weren't you briefed that the President did not authorize a monetary payment? Malloy asked.

"Not until I was already airborne in the C-130 bound for Shiraz." I answered. "I had decided I wasn't going to leave any money for him anyway. I planned on getting all of us out of the country before telling General Rashid where to find the money. I at one time thought about getting a satchel full of monopoly money to leave him, but I figured that might piss him - oops! Sorry sir. It might anger him even more." That at least got a big chuckle out of everyone. "As it turned out sir, once the Iranians made the C-130 turn and burn out of there, I knew the money was a moot point. We were in for a helicopter raid and a fire fight."

"Well captain, I guess you dodged a bullet on that one." Malloy said. "It's hard to tell how it would have come down here had you actually pulled off the bluff."

"So how did it happen that five Iranian nationals came out with you all?" This was NS Advisor Mike Nash.

I took a deep breath, glanced at Colonel Watson and Speedball, saw that neither of them was going to speak up, so "I guess that was my doing as well sir." I said meekly. "The Iranian captain that was my contact had been one of my students in flight training at Laughlin AFB a while back, and we struck up a friendship. He had me over for dinner a couple times in Shiraz and he introduced me to his father, the two star in charge of the operation at the base. General Ranjahni actually flew with me on one of our training sorties. The idea of...."

"Who authorized that? A foreign national flying in one of our jets?" It was Air Force Chief of Staff Furman. "Was that your idea Watson?"

"Yes sir, I guess it was, except that they didn't fly in our jet." The boss replied and explained. "Captain Mitchell flew in the back seat of the general in one of the Iranian jets. And no sir, I did not get approval from on high for that." General Bong threw a hard glance at Colonel Watson for his tone.

"Communications in and out of Shiraz during this exercise were spotty at best." Bong said in our defense. The general showed up to fly and he wanted to fly with Mitchell. From what I understand he was very impressed."

"OK. OK, fine but how does all this authorize an asylum ride out? Nash asked.

"Sir, Captain Ranjahni came up with that out of the blue to me." I responded. "He was convinced that he didn't want to raise his kids in the upcoming environment in Iran. His wife is an ex Miss Iran, and a very westernized woman. Jani, er Captain Ranjahni feared that she would be treated as a pariah under the

Muslim extremist regime, and he also wanted to get his father freed. His mother, her mother and sister and two kids also got out by fishing vessel. There evidently wasn't room for more folks on the boat. By this time the general had been placed under arrest and confined to his office. The bottom line though was that Captain Ranjahni basically threatened to expose what he knew about our plans if I didn't agree to take them out."

"How much did he know of the plans?" It was Durkee. "Had you told him what you were going to do?"

"Sir, this is where I come in." Speedball finally came to the rescue. "Captain Mitchell came to me with this dilemma and I basically told him we would not help in any way, but since there was room on the helicopters, if his friends could get themselves to us, we'd take them out. He had not divulged any of the plan to the Iranian, and especially since Captain Ranjahni himself was getting ready to fly, we expected it would never come to fruition. It was a complete surprise to us when the wife got out of a car and started shooing her kids towards the choppers. I will admit we did help her though. One of their forces was about to blow her shit - er.. stuff away and one of our snipers took him and his buddy out."

"We were even more surprised when the captain and his father showed up on Mitchell's wing asking to join up as we were egressing the area." Colonel Watson piped in. "When their own missile shot them down I thought it was not an issue, and it wouldn't have been had it not been for the quick thinking of one of the F-15 pilots and the proximity of our rescue choppers."

I completed the saga of the evening and we answered a few more questions. "Ok gentlemen. Thanks very much. I will brief the President. To be honest, I don't know if he will look at this whole incident as as a heroic venture or as an unfortunate episode creating bad blood with one of our former allies." SECDEF Malloy said. "Speedball, we're sending one of the CIAs exec jets to bring your team back to D.C. The rest of you go about your business, but standby for further inquiries."

By the time the call was over it was too late for us to launch for home, so we checked into billeting and then hit the Officers' Club. The Tango team and General Bong joined us and it was a typical fighter pilot night at the Club. General Bong especially was in a good mood. He wanted to know all the details of both the mission and our 6 weeks in Shiraz. He had a lot of good war stories from his Vietnam War days. He had some great stories about his father's exploits as America's #1 Ace in WWII as well. Most of us sat around gawking and wishing we had been around back then.

CHAPTER THIRTY FOUR

AGAIN?

The next morning I went directly to base operations to file our flight plan to Aviano. The plan was to get there early enough to turn and get home by about 4 PM. As I walked into the building my "brick" went off in its beeper mode. It was Lt. Colonel Watson. "Griz, hold off on the flight plan and get your ass down to the command post. We got a problem, and if Speedball and his guys are there tell them to abort too."

"What's up boss?" I asked.

"Our helicopters are overdue. There was a Mayday call last night about midnight, picked up by a transient C-5 and it sounds like they are down somewhere in Syria." Watson explained. "Just get over here. and find those Tango guys."

As it turned out, Speedball and his group were just climbing onto their fancy executive jet. I borrowed a truck from the Base Ops folks and sped out to them. In a half hour I was in the command post with Speedball, Watson, General Bong, and BG Blackburn, the Incirlik Wing Commander.

"Glad we could catch you all before you left, but it looks like we have another rescue operation here," Said General Bong, "Although this time we need to rescue the rescuers. Bring us up to speed Tom." He gestured to General Blackburn.

"Yes sir." Blackburn flashed up a map of Syria, centered on an area about 150 miles south of Incirlik. "Gentlemen, it looks like we have two choppers down in the desert about here." He pointed to the map. "The Mayday call picked up by the C-5 guys was fairly descriptive. They gave a TACAN cut and said something about surface to air missiles. If they were in this area they were really close to some Syrian army troops that have been in a conflict with the Kurds in this vicinity here." He described the order of battle in the area and the conflict between the Kurds and the Syrians. "The Syrians have SA-7 missiles they got from the Soviets."

TACAN stands for Tactical Air Navigation. It is an ultra high frequency beacon from which aircraft can read azimuth and distance from the sight. So if the chopper pilot said he was on the 270 radial for 40 miles, it meant he was 40 miles due west of the TACAN beacon. In this case, the beacon he used was at the airport at Raqqa, a city in the middle of Syria.

And here I thought this long nightmare was over, but there was no way we would leave Wop and Red Baron and their crews out there in the desert in what could be hostile territory.

"I've tasked a Recce mission to make a pass over the area. They should be there in about an hour." General Bong checked his watch. Fortunately there was a flight of RF-4s on the ramp at Incirlik, down on a training deployment from their base at Alconbury RAFB, England, and having the USAFE Commander in Chief on base made the tasking hard to refuse. The RF-4 is the reconnaissance version of the F-4, equipped with a variety of cameras in the nose that could take good photos while on a high speed dash through the territory. There were also two HH-53 helicopters on the Incirlik ramp. They were part of the squadron that was helping the Kurds, and as soon as they heard the fate of their squadron mates they wanted to be in on a rescue.

We adjourned to a separate office in the Incirlik Command Center. General Bong put Lt. Col. Watson in charge of the operation, but he and General Blackburn stayed close to add any "advice" and instruction they could. Speedball and his Tango Team let us know that they were here to help and would be whatever special ops force we needed. Rhino and Bear Gablewski retrieved what maps there were of the area thought to be the location of the downed choppers, and General Blackburn tasked his wing intelligence folks to help. In the meantime, Tony Gilford took charge of getting our jets fueled and armed. We decided to go with Cluster Bomb Units (CBU) again because it didn't look like there were any structures in the area requiring hard bombs, and the CBU would be best against troops and vehicles.

The Recce crew returned after about an hour and down loaded their photos. They also joined us in the planning room with some very valuable intel. It seems that one of the guys in the Jolly flight came up on the radio when the RF-4 made their first pass. The pilot was able to get them onto a more private frequency and learned that Wop and Gronk were dead. Their chopper had blown up in mid air after the missile hit. Baron and Snoopy were able to auto-rotate their bird in for a hard landing, and it was totaled as well. Red Baron was ok. Snoopy has a broken leg and some bruised ribs. The Recce crew said there were forces due south of the wreckage about 10 miles, likely the ones who shot the choppers down. He said there was also a rag-tag group of fighters only about 4 miles east of the choppers. The intel folks allowed as how those were probably Kurdish forces and showed us on the map their last known locations in the area. He also told us that he might be able to communicate with the Kurds through contacts they were using in Incirlik to support the helicopter relief missions that were being conducted. That was big news.

Basically the Kurds controlled land east and north of the Euphrates River, and more specifically between the border of Turkey and about 100 miles south, pretty much bordered on the west by a major north-south highway between the border and the city of Raqqa. They were trying to take over the huge dam that formed the Assad Reservoir at the town of Madinat ath Thawrah. However, it was heavily guarded by Syrian forces. It looked like the planned route of flight for the choppers was south to north and several miles east of the reservoir, and over Kurdish held territory. With the inputs provided by the helicopter pilots Rhino and Bear picked a route of flight down to the wreckage sight that would follow the road to Raqqa, but a few miles east over desolate desert, not over the populated road or towns.

There were three Kurdish liaison officers on base at Incirlik. They helped coordinate the relief efforts, and they knew the area very well. We enlisted two of them to go with us on the choppers on this mission. They were able to link up communications via phone and radio to the Kurds at their command center closer to the damn. Basically it was a phone call to a guy with a radio near the border, and radio transmissions from him to another fighter who had phone connection to the nearest fighters. Needless to say it took a while for a call to go through and back. We were able to at least get the Kurds moving toward the crash site to attempt to rescue the downed crew, and we alerted them there would be a force inbound to recover them in a few hours.

We held a mass briefing in one of the squadron buildings at Incirlik at one o'clock. General Bong and General Blackburn were both there. Colonel Watson had the podium. The first thing he said in his gruff voice was, "Are there any God Damned reporters in this room?" Everyone looked around. Seeing none, the boss went on, "Good, then I don't want to hear of any Washington Post or even Incirlik Base Newspaper story about this operation, at least not until after it's over." That got a chuckle out of everyone, even though Watson was deadly serious.

Watson briefed the general plan. The two HH-53s would take off at 3 PM and head directly for the border a few miles east of the highway leading to Raqqa. Speedball, and the entire Tango Team would be on board, split up between the two birds. One of the Kurdish liaisons would be on each helicopter as well. We would launch off in our Phantoms about an hour later. Colonel Watson would lead one flight of four, Tony Gilford the second. Rhino and I would be number three in the first flight. The plan was for the first four ship of F-4s to blow straight through to the rescue area keeping low to avoid Syrian radar. Our mission was to blow over the site and hopefully Red Baron would be up on the radio. If there were any troops in contact, we would set up a low level orbit and lend close air support. If they were not in conflict right there, we would continue on to where the Syrians were and take the fight to them, spreading our CBU around, sparing no one that looked to be an organized army.

Tony's flight was to set up an orbit offset the choppers to lend them any help they might need on the way in or out. Once the rescuers got to the crash site, Tony and flight would set up an orbit to be able to react at short notice to any incoming fire the choppers might get. Our flight then, once we expended our bombs, would climb out to a higher altitude above shoulder fired missile range and swing to air to air, looking for any Syrian MIG traffic that may be called in. We would move our Combat Air Patrol (CAP) site north as the choppers moved north, to cross the border back into Turkey at about the same time.

That was the plan. I love it when a plan comes together. Not today! Jollys (Three and Four) took off on time, but about 15 minutes out Jolly Four had an engine overheat and he had to put it down quickly in a flat area. Jolly Three landed beside him and everyone but the pilot of the wounded bird jumped on the good bird. The pilot stayed with his aircraft to keep scavengers away until help could come from Incirlik. That maneuver didn't take too long - maybe ten minutes, but it was an omen of things to come.

The Sabers took off on time, but missing one. Number Two in Tony's flight had flight control issues and never got airborne, so he had a three ship to escort just one chopper. Saber One flight blew by the Jolly just after we crossed into Syria. We stayed down low in a box formation. The boss got Red Baron up on the radio.

They had a handful of Kurds with them, but the main force had fallen back. They were under attack from three sides by Syrian army regulars.

"Green em' up Sabers, set up for singles, check flares." The Boss was calling for us to arm our sytems and to set up for only a single bomb release at a time. He expected to be here for a while, selectively picking our targets to keep the bad guys off the good guys. He also wanted to set our chaff/flare dispensers up to fire flares out if we saw any SA-7 heat seeking shoulder fired missiles. Hopefully the flares would pull the missile off our tailpipes. We all acknowledged, "Two, Three, Four." We climbed up to about 1500 feet as we got closer so we could see ahead and have room to dive down and drop on our first pass.

Sure enough, there were soldiers, jeeps, armored personnel carriers (APCs), even a couple tanks. "Three, take the right flank, we've got the left." Watson ordered my element to attack the eastern flank of the site. I followed his lead, dumped the nose over, picked up some troops and a jeep in my sight and presented them with lots of bomblets for gifts. Saber Four followed my lead. We broke hard left after the pass, picked up number two in front and followed them around in a low level box pattern. This time we laid four singles along the closest line of troops south of the choppers.

"Good shootin' Sabers." Baron yelled. Keep 'em coming. They're closing in on our east flank."

"Roger that." Watson answered, "extending out a bit on this one Sabers, then attack from the south." He wanted to go after the east flank of the site, but not deliver our bombs directly over the heads of the good guys. We made two passes on that general heading, but in doing so we were flying over the bulk of the enemy force to the south. Because we were so low they didn't have time to track us, but they did fire off a couple missiles in futility. Watson had enough of that and he moved the pattern back toward the north.

Just then, "Saber, Jolly 3's at your 10 o'clock low ready to approach." We had to break off that pattern.

"Roger Jolly, Saber One's breaking east. Break Break, Saber 11 we'll stay east of the north south line, you stay west. Cleared in hot." The Boss told Tony where to set up his pattern and we would maintain separation by an imaginary line north-south that the Jolly flew in on.

"Saber 11 copies." Tony acknowledged.

We made two more passes and cleared any movement we could see east of the site. Then the Boss zoomed up high, pumping flares. "Saber 1's Winchester, swinging to air to air. Saber 11 you got it all. We'll come back with guns if necessary." We each followed our leader up, pumping flares as we flew through the envelope of the SA-7. There were a couple shots taken, but I don't think they ever even reached the flares. We set up a mile behind the lead element and Boomer (Saber 4) joined to a fighting wing on me. I switched to heat seeking missiles, and Rhino dove into the radar looking for playmates.

Jolly 3 roared into the site and planted himself right next to the downed birds. Speed ball and his gang dove out and took up defensive positions. They were getting incoming rifle and mortar fire from due south. Some of it was really close, too close for a CBU bomblet dispersal, so after three bomb passes Tony had his guys come in from the west with guns a-blazin.' They honked it back around and came in from the east on another pass, then Tony called out "Winchester rifle," meaning their guns were empty. Two good passes with the guns in an F-4 or F-15 is about all you get, but with four of them spraying high explosive round around, it was effective.

The Kurds had witnessed all of this and after jumping up and down and cheering with every pass we made, they decided to take advantage of the situation and moved in. They surrounded the crash site and were able to hold off anymore close in threats while Jolly 3 got everybody aboard, including the bodies of Wop and Gronk. During all this time, Stinker had wired both the crippled choppers with several packets of C-4. He set a timer device between the two and when it looked like Jolly 3 was ready to blow this popsicle stand, he initiated the timer for 3 minutes. One of the liaison Kurds told the others to back away from the choppers while Stinker climbed aboard, and the helicopter lifted off, swung around and did just that - headed north. Tony and his flight made two more bomb passes to drop their last rounds of CBU and then followed the Jolly out as the escort. The downed choppers blew up in an impressive explosion, spreading helicopter parts over several acres of Syrian desert.

Meanwhile, back at the ranch, up at 10,000' we were watching the show and looking for Migs. Try as we might we couldn't will any to come play. This whole operation from when we had blown across on the first pass to when Jolly and Tony's flight were off to the north only took six minutes, so unless the Syrians knew we might be there, they wouldn't have had time to scramble to help they're comrades out. We thought.

As we headed north in our box formation at about 10,000' Romanski in Boomer's pit picked up a glint of sun off something back at our left 7 o'clock. "Four's got a bogey, 7 o'clock, five miles, a little high." Boomer said on the radio. I checked left about 15 degrees to pick up the tally. In the meantime, the Boss dumped the nose and accelerated.

"Let's boogie boys. Push it up." Watson called, knowing it's always better to leave a fight that's no threat than to hang around and get into something we might regret. I broke back to the right behind him, dumped the nose and pushed the power up to full military (without afterburner). My little jink maneuver had put us about two miles in trail, so I lit a couple stages of the burner to catch up. I thought Boomer would do the same. However, both he and J.J. had their heads on a swivel looking for the intruder. They fell further behind.

"Four, push it up." I called. He heard, and he did…. push it up to full afterburner to catch me. Bad move. It turned out to be a Mig 21 Fishbed that must have been doing the speed of heat to catch us, and our little maneuver to see him helped solve his equation. He had closed to within a mile dead six to Boomer.

"Four break right, flares." Rhino called out. He'd seen a missile come off the rail of the Mig. Boomer broke hard right and pumped out a couple flares. I broke hard as well. As it turned out, so did Colonel Watson and Bosco. The Mig was coming in hot, so when Boomer made his hard turn the Syrian slid into an overshoot but also cranked into a turn. Boomer saw him now and held his turn as much as he could, probably 6 Gs. He had rolled his power back to idle at the break call to decrease the heat source for the missile, but now he was slowing down quickly and he knew he didn't want to get into a slow speed "knife fight" with a MIG 21. He pushed the power up to military and then full afterburner. Doing that when the F-4 has slowed down and is in a high angle of attack will often cause a compressor stall in the engines. He couldn't afford that, so he knew to be gentle with this power increase. Quickly however, Boomer and JJ were in a nose high, slow speed turning engagement with the Syrian who had slid to the outside of the turn and was falling back.

A slow speed dogfight is not a horse race. You don't want to be the one out in front. It's the guy behind who gets the first, and probably last shot. Unfortunately though, unless you have wingmen as well - someone else on your side, and you don't pay attention to your target's friends, you have probably made yourself the ham in a ham sandwich. Rhino and I looked hard for any other enemy aircraft out there, finding it hard to believe this one MIG driver would risk attacking four F-4s, or four of anything, all by his lonesome. We didn't see anything, so my goal was to real quickly complete that ham sandwich and free Boomer of his nemesis. Watson and Bosco had the same thoughts, so there we were, five high speed jets in a tight "fur ball," separated by only hundreds of feet.

Actually only three of us were "high speed." Boomer and the MIG pilot had decelerated to just above stall speed, and even with the slats the F-4E has, the characteristics of the Phantom in a stall were to the advantage of the MIG. The F-4 will fall off the climbing turn naturally to try to find flying airspeed. The Fishbed can basically stay in that nose up attitude and do a "death dance" while its prey falls over in front of him. At that point, all the MIG pilot has to do is step on a rudder pedal and let his nose track down to perfect gun parameters on the Phantom, or he can let the F-4 separate a little more so that he is in missile parameters. They weren't quite at that phase yet when the three of us had them out in front.

The threat I had was to not shoot the good guy. Even with a heat seeker lock on the MIG, it would be easy for it to switch to the double afterburner of the F-4 as they basically do a dance in front of us. I wanted to keep my speed up and I saw that Boomer was holding him off for now, so I blasted by and turned hard to get in parameters the next time around. The Boss and Bosco had a larger perspective and Watson must have had the same thought as I did - not wanting to transfer lock onto the wrong target. Bosco however, smelled his second kill of the campaign and he let a heat seeker fly. Good shot. Direct hit and the MIG 21 exploded in our faces and in Boomer's mirror.

Watson came up on the radio. "Ok, Sabers let's knock it off. I'm heading to the north, join to tactical." None of us said anything. Bosco slid into position on his leader and I fell back using the spacing to give Boomer time to accelerate and join on me. We kept the speed up and altitude down on the deck until we crossed the border into Turkey. We came up on the chopper and Tony's flight about that time and we all went in to Incirlik together.

That night at the Incirlik bar was a little subdued. Although there was a tendency to want to celebrate Bosco's kill, there was the overlying fact that we had lost Wop and Gronk, and Bosco wasn't quite sure if he'd done the right thing by taking a shot his squadron commander wouldn't take. He and Boomer, J.J. and FUBAR all huddled together and there were some high fives and smiles, and nothing more was said…. for now.

The next day our trip back to Hahn was uneventful. We did hop through Aviano and arrived in Germany about 1600 hours, only to find the weather had gone down again at Hahn. We landed at Bitburg Air Base and waited for the inevitable Blue Goose to take us home. Everyone but me. Pete Trask met me at my jet when I landed with a cold Bitburger Beer and dragged me over to his house for the night. I made it back to Hahn a day later.

CHAPTER THIRTY FIVE
WASHINGTON

Detective Duke Welch decided to confront Major Tyler at his office and to try and keep the Major's relationship with Marianne Rodgers withheld from his wife for now. After all, there was no evidence that Marianne's swan dive was at the hands of Tyler. He went to the Pentagon to the offices of the Secretary of Defense and asked to see Tyler. After about 15 minutes a young man appeared and allowed as how Tyler had not come in to work today. They had called his home to see if he was all right, but his wife had no clue. As far as she knew he had left for work on time this morning. Welch identified himself to the aide and suggested that Tyler is a "person of interest" in Marianne's death, and asked to see Tyler's office. The aide disappeared back into the bowels of the offices. A few minutes later Secretary of Defense Lawrence Malloy came out of his office and approached Welch. "What's this about Tyler being mixed up in that she devil reporter's suicide? Does this have anything to do with the disappearance of the President's Chief of Staff?" Malloy asked.

"It very well might sir. Mr. Taggart was found dead yesterday - an apparent murder, and we know that the good major here had a soiree with Miss Rodgers one afternoon last week, and a run in with Mr. Taggart the next evening while in the company of Miss Rodgers." Welch explained. "I simply want to ask him a few questions. Since he is not here, and apparently not at home, I thought perhaps I could find something in his office that might shed light on where he might be."

"Taggart is dead?" Welch couldn't tell if the Secretary was happy or sad. "Does the President know?"

"I have no idea sir. The case is under the jurisdiction of the Surry County, Virginia Sheriff's Office." The detective answered. "I assume they will make the appropriate notifications. Now," He gestured toward the door to Tyler's office, "would it be ok if I took a look around?"

Malloy thought about that for a minute and as he was about to speak, Major Tyler came in dressed in his AF blues. "Good morning sir. Sorry I'm a little late. I stopped by to get my car washed. It got pretty slopped up with the rain yesterday."

"Good morning Tom. No problem. This detective here has some questions for you." Malloy responded. "Did you know about Bobby Taggart's death?"

Tyler turned pale as a ghost. He looked at Welch and then back at Malloy. "Er, no sir. Taggart? That's the President's Chief of Staff? Um, Detective Welch right? I told you what I know about Taggart and Miss Rodgers the other day."

"Tom, why don't you and the detective go into your office. This is hardly the place for these discussions." Malloy obviously wanted to get any notion of a scandal out of the public view of his outer office.

Tyler led Welch into his office and closed the door. He suddenly became very defensive and cold. "Have a seat detective. I'm not sure I can help you." Welch looked around the room very quickly. His eyes rested on an object on the credenza behind the major's desk. He sat down and asked, "So tell me Major, your car. Did it have a lot of mud on one side from driving through a mud hole down near Surry a couple nights ago?"

"Uh, I don't think it was any one place on the car. It was just real dirty. Surry, Virginia?" Tyler responded. "I'm not sure I even know where that is."

Welch stood up and leaned forward, putting his palms n the major's desk. "Where that is Major is where you got that bookend there behind you the night before last. Now, I want you to stand up and walk around here and put your hands on this desk just the way I have mine now. I don't think you want to make a big fuss right now, but you are under arrest. You have the right to remain silent,.."

"Under arrest? I don't think so." Tyler jumped to his feet. He had a Glock nine millimeter automatic in his hand, aimed dead center on the detective's chest. "Now, you stand up straight and very slowly take your weapon out and put it on the desk." Welch did as he said.

"Now, slide it over here to me, nice and easy." Welch did. "Good, now assume that position again - palms on the desk, feet spread and out behind you." Welch did as he was told. Tyler came around and patted him down, finding only his radio and badge and wallet. He pulled the radio out and threw it on the desk.

"Now, stand up and walk nice and steady out the door, through the outer office and into the hall. I'll be right behind you with this gun under my coat aimed at your back. We're going to leave the building and go for a ride."

Welch walked to the door, opened it and stepped out towards the outer door. "Miriam, I'm going to show the detective out, I'll be right......" Tyler started to talk to the receptionist, then stopped abruptly. Four U.S. Marines were standing dead center in the room, all toting weapons, though not drawn. "What's going on?" Tyler asked. Then he saw Secretary Malloy standing in the doorway to his office with a disgusted look on his face. Tyler stopped, then pushed Welch hard against the closest Marine, and bolted back into his office locking the door.

Welch recovered and said, "Thanks guys." Then to the closed door. "Major Taggart, don't make this any more difficult than it already is." He tried the door handle. The marines drew their weapons. Miriam dug through her desk drawer and produced a key and handed it to Welch. "Ok. Thanks ma'am. Now find a nice safe spot to hide. Take the Secretary with you."

"Tyler. I have a key. We're coming in." Welch said then stepped aside from in front of the door. Just in time. The major fired off three rounds into the door, splintering it. The rounds imbedded in the opposite wall, only two feet from Malloy, still standing in his own doorway. He ducked inside quickly, pulling Miriam with him. Welch reached around from the side and inserted the spare key, then, "Blam!" a single shot rang out from within.

The first Marine hit the door like a linebacker, almost knocking it off its hinges. Welch followed him with the other three jarheads right behind. Tyler was laying on the floor behind his desk, half of his head missing, Glock in one hand and a bookend statue of a horse's head in the other.

Welch thanked the marines. They had been on the doors downstairs when he entered the Pentagon. He had to show them his weapon and give it up as he went through the metal detector. But then he told them what he was here for and that they might want to come along to the SECDEF's office. Probably only because it was the SECDEF's office did they oblige.

EPILOGUE

Shah Pahlavi had been asking the U.S. for entry into the country for treatment to his cancer. President Carver hemmed and hawed and delayed, especially since the radicals in Tehran vehemently objected, demonstrating in front of the American embassy, burning the U.S. flag in the streets, and rioting against their own city. Since the military had been basically shoved aside by the new leader, Ayatollah Khomeini, they pretty much stood by and did nothing. After our escape and successful rescue of our people, things got even worse. Supposedly for that reason it was decided not to celebrate in any way our success. So, in small celebrations at the recipients' home bases awards and medals were quietly handed out.

Rhino, Major Shivner, and the two helicopter crews were awarded the Silver Star, WOP's and Gronk's posthumously. Shivner also got a Purple Heart. Trask, the C-130 pilot and copilot, and yours truly each got a Bronze Star. The rest of the military members got Air Medals, basically because they flew a "combat mission," and the Tango team members were awarded the civilian equivalent. They and the UDTs were simply handed a medal and as usual, their names were never publicized for doing anything.

The Shah was granted permission to enter the country on October 29, 1979, but it was too late and he died on November second. The Iranians went on the rampage again. They wanted his body returned, probably to be paraded around and burned at the stake. They also campaigned to get the millions of dollars that were in different accounts owned by the Shah returned to Iran. None of that happened, and on the 4th of November radical students and Muslim extremist stormed the American embassy, ripped down the flag and held the whole staff hostage. President Carver and his senior staff had many discussions amongst themselves and the Ambassador in Tehran, but the President opted to do nothing to thwart the takeover, and sat on the whole issue for months. The Iranians did release 13 people in mid November, women and African Americans, but they kept 52 embassy staff for 444 days until January, 1981.

Finally, in April of 1980, Carver authorized a rescue attempt proposed by his Defense Department and others. Operation Eagle Claw was launched with 8 RH-53 helicopters from the aircraft Carrier USS Nimitz and C-130s, landing on a salt flat called Desert One in Iran at night. Two helicopters had maintenance issues and returned to the Nimitz, and a third was inoperable after landing in the desert. It was determined that the mission could not be accomplished with just five choppers and the mission was aborted. In the departure from Desert One a helicopter ran into one of the C-130s, destroying both and killing 8 Americans and one Iranian civilian, injuring 3 others. The remainder of the force was evacuated and 5 helicopters were abandoned (a Gift for the Iranians). The mission was widely described as a disaster and a debacle, and was a major issue in that year's presidential election campaign.

Ronald Reagan was swept into office that November and on the day of his inauguration - January 20, 1981, the embassy staff was released. As a direct result of the aborted rescue mission where much of the blame was pointed toward the lack of communication and coordination amongst the military branches, the Special Operations Command was created and established for future operations.

Jim "Rhino" Reiner was selected for a pilot training position from which he graduated with honors and ended up flying the new F-16 Fighting Falcon. Pete Trask worked through the ranks at Bitburg and was eventually assigned to Langley AFB, Virginia as the Squadron Commander of the 48 TFS air defense squadron, flying the F-15.

Major General Ranjahni, his wife, mother-in-law, and wife's sister and children basically disappeared, likely placed into a witness protection program with another name and a new domicile. There evidently were a couple of failed attempts by persons unknown to capture and assassinate the General, but so far none successful. Jani wasn't as lucky. He and his family settled in Dallas, Texas and Jani got on with American Airlines. One day about a year after the action, Jani's wife and two children were killed in a car bomb. Jani was off on a trip, and thus unharmed. He made it his life's purpose to avenge the loss of his family and went to work for the CIA. He basically disappeared for all intents and purposes to me or any who knew him.

I left Hahn in June, '79 to a staff position at Tactical Air Command Headquarters at Langley AFB, Virginia. There I ended up as the Executive Officer to the two-star Director of Operations.

I left Langley three years later and upgraded to the F-16. After three years at Sumter, S.C. flying the Viper at Shaw AFB, I went to Korea and was selected to command the 80th TFS Headhunters at Kunsan, the scene of the next great adventure. Stay tuned for "Tremble."

THE END

ABOUT THE AUTHOR

Colonel Dana Duthie's career as an Air Force fighter pilot is the basis for many of the experiences in "Phantoms of the Shah" His Air Force career spanned 24 years, from pilot training in Georgia and instructor in Texas to the skies over Southeast Asia, and from the F-4 phantom in Germany to the F-16 Falcon in South Carolina, Korea and Germany. The theme of "Phantom" spawned from his tour with the 10th Tactical Fighter Squadron in Germany flying the F-4 during 1975-79. He also "paid his dues" with three headquarters assignments and professional schooling. Colonel Duthie retired in 1992. He lives in Broomfield and Steamboat Springs, Colorado with his wife, and two children and four grandchildren nearby. One grandson is currently assigned to the USS Carl Vinson, nuclear carrier in the Pacific.

FROM THE SAME AUTHOR

Phantoms of the Shah is the third book published by Colonel Dana Duthie, USAF (Ret). It is actually the second of four adventures in the Air Force career of Brad Mitchell. Thus **Phantoms** is a prequel to **Tremble** and **Dark Rain.**

Tremble is based on the author's tour in Korea in 1985-86 and Mitchell is the squadron Commander of the 80th Tactical Fighter Squadron. North Korea has stepped over the line one time too many and the Air Force launches an attack on a suspected nuclear weapons site in the North, and attempts to rescue a team of international weapons inspectors.

Dark Rain centers on the last years of Brad Mitchell's career as he participates in quelling Iranian terrorist attacks on the U.S. An Iranian "mole" steals an F-16 fighter armed with a nuclear bomb and flies it to a base in Libya with the intention of using it in an attack on Israel. **Dark Rain** is the story of how the U.S. goes about recovering the jet and its weapon and stopping the Iranian tourist attacks.

Hopefully there will be a fourth book centered on the early years of the author's career. In the meantime, don't miss the trilogy, available in hard and soft back as well as an e-book.